Memories stirred...

Through the endless sleepless nights, she had yearned for the comfort of his long, warm body, and the closeness they'd once shared. For an instant Dana leaned into Cody's embrace, unable to stop herself.

His hand ran up her back to her neck and he wrapped his fingers around her nape, his thumb tracing her jaw. She lifted her head, caught in a dream of her own making, believing she could have just this one kiss, and then go back to her orderly life without a regret.

His mouth touched hers, the taste and feel so familiar, so welcome, it made her want to cry. She shivered.

"Cody, I'm not sure we should do this."

His mouth came back to hers and he kissed her again, stealing her breath, her will.

"What should we be doing, then?" he muttered, his breath warm on her lips. "Arguing about the best way to keep you alive?"

Dear Harlequin Intrigue Reader,

Yet again we have a power-packed lineup of fantastic books for you this month, starting with the second story in the new Harlequin continuity series TRUEBLOOD, TEXAS. *Secret Bodyguard* by B.J. Daniels brings together an undercover cop and a mobster's daughter in a wary alliance in order to find her baby. But will they find a family together before all is said and done?

Ann Voss Peterson contributes another outstanding legal thriller to Harlequin Intrigue with *His Witness, Her Child*. Trust me, there's nothing sexier than a cowboy D.A. who's as tough as nails on criminals, yet is as tender as lamb's wool with women and children. Except...

One of Julie Miller's Taylor men! This month read about brother Brett Taylor in *Sudden Engagement*. Mystery, matchmaking—it's all part and parcel for any member of THE TAYLOR CLAN.

Finally, I'm thrilled to introduce you to Mallory Kane, who debuts at Harlequin Intrigue with *The Lawman Who Loved Her*. Hang on to your hat—and your heart. This story—and this hunky hero—will blow you away.

Round up all four! And be on the lookout next month for a *new* Harlequin Intrigue trilogy by Amanda Stevens called EDEN'S CHILDREN.

Happy reading,

Denise O'Sullivan
Associate Senior Editor
Harlequin Intrigue

THE LAWMAN
WHO LOVED HER

MALLORY KANE

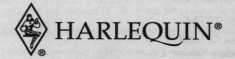

HARLEQUIN®

TORONTO • NEW YORK • LONDON
AMSTERDAM • PARIS • SYDNEY • HAMBURG
STOCKHOLM • ATHENS • TOKYO • MILAN • MADRID
PRAGUE • WARSAW • BUDAPEST • AUCKLAND

ISBN 0-373-22620-9

THE LAWMAN WHO LOVED HER

Copyright © 2001 by Rickey R. Mallory

Printed in U.S.A.

ABOUT THE AUTHOR

Mallory Kane worked in the medical field for many years before leaving to make time for her other loves, writing and art. She loves romance and suspense, and two of her favorite things are dangerous heroes and dauntless heroines. She lives in Mississippi with her husband and their two dauntless cats.

She would be delighted to hear from readers. You can write to her c/o Harlequin Books, 300 East 42nd Street, Sixth Floor, New York, NY 10017.

Books by Mallory Kane

HARLEQUIN INTRIGUE
620—THE LAWMAN WHO LOVED HER

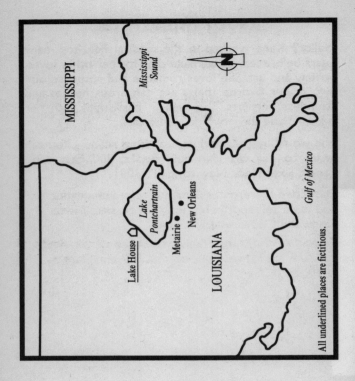

MISSISSIPPI

Mississippi Sound

LOUISIANA

Lake Pontchartrain

Lake House

Metairie ●
● New Orleans

Gulf of Mexico

All underlined places are fictitious.

CAST OF CHARACTERS

Dana Charles Maxwell—She divorced Cody to protect her heart. Now he's back, and she's running for her life.

Detective Cody Maxwell—His job is everything to Cody, or so he thinks, until a killer threatens the one person who means more to him than his own life.

Gerard Fontenot—The diabolical killer vowed to make Cody pay for what he'd done. Now neither Cody nor his wife are safe.

Detective Devereaux Gautier—The intimidating cop has a soft spot in his heart for his best friend, Cody, and Cody's wife.

Captain Hamilton—While the police captain heads the hunt for Fontenot, he sends Cody and Dana to safety, he thinks.

This one is for the intrepid critiquers, Lorraine,
Debbie and especially Sherri, who has already said,
"I told you so."

Prologue

Gerard Fontenot stood in the shadows, in an alley off St. Peter Street, waiting. Waiting was something he understood. He didn't like it, but he could do it. He had waited for four years to be here tonight. And while he waited, he'd planned.

A small smile played around his thin lips. Detective Maxwell had underestimated him. They all had. They couldn't pin his wife's murder on him, although Maxwell had tried. For some reason, he had taken Fontenot's case as a personal vendetta. He'd dogged Fontenot's footsteps until he'd nearly driven him crazy.

Shooting Maxwell four years ago had been a foolish mistake, caused by Maxwell getting too close. Maxwell had almost blundered onto the truth about Fontenot's wife's death.

No more mistakes. He'd learned patience and control in prison. He'd perfected his plans and honed his hatred to razor sharpness. He'd always known he was smarter. Now he was invincible. No one could touch him now.

He was playing with Maxwell, toying with him like a cat with a mouse, and the results were already more than he could have hoped. It was a brilliant maneuver to involve Maxwell's ex-wife. Brilliant. Maxwell was spooked. Fontenot could tell. The detective knew what he was up to, but he couldn't do anything about it.

Fontenot's smile widened as Maxwell's Laser pulled up to the curb. The detective unfolded his lanky frame from the car, and glanced around. Fontenot stood absolutely still, relishing the tingling excitement as Maxwell's gaze flickered past the shadowed alley in which he stood.

His heartbeat accelerated and a bead of sweat limned his upper lip as Maxwell disappeared into the stairwell leading to his upstairs apartment. Although Fontenot could no longer see him, his mind counted out each step, each action, as Maxwell moved inevitably toward his destiny.

Fontenot didn't move a muscle, didn't breathe. His muscles tensed, and his groin tightened in anticipation as sweetly agonizing as slow, drawn-out foreplay. He waited.

Chapter One

By the time Cody's brain registered what he'd heard, it was too late. He threw himself sideways with every ounce of strength he commanded, but it wasn't enough. His head hit first, and slid as his shoulder slammed into the hardwood floor. For a few seconds, the quiet, ominous click echoed in his ears, seeming louder than the explosion which followed.

He lay, tense and still, listening for any sound that would tell him his attacker was still there. Nothing. The building was quiet, now that the echo of the gunshot had faded. Down the hall, he heard a door slam. His mouth turned up. *Thanks, neighbor*. Good thing he wasn't hurt. Cautiously, he reached for his gun, and his left shoulder screamed with pain.

Too slow. Dev and the other guys would give him hell for being too slow to dodge a bullet. Dana would be terrified.

He winced at that unguarded thought. No she wouldn't. She wasn't part of his life anymore. He sat up slowly and took stock of his condition. Nasty bump on his forehead, painful scrape on his cheek. Bullet wound in his shoulder. From the way it felt, he guessed the bullet had gone clean through the meaty part of his bicep. He turned his head and saw the mark on the wall. Yep.

He stood, and swayed with unexpected dizziness. His left arm didn't want to work, and he could feel blood, hot and sticky, wetting his sweatshirt. He glanced down. *Damn.* His leather jacket was ruined.

Cody pulled out his cell phone and nudged it open with his chin. He pressed a fast-dial button and leaned against the wall, praying that his partner hadn't let his cell phone battery go down.

"Dev? Hey, man. I need some…help." Cody blinked against the blackness that was seeping in from the edge of his vision and looked at the kitchen chair, which had been positioned directly in front of the door.

"Help? How'd you manage to get in trouble in the past fifteen minutes? What's up?" Detective Devereaux Gautier's voice was tinged with amusement.

"Well, I've got a situation. At my apartment. Can you get over here right away and call it in?"

"Situation? You okay?" His partner's voice immediately became professionally crisp.

"Yeah, I'm okay," he said wryly. "Just a flesh wound. Fontenot booby-trapped my door. Listen, man, I'm afraid he may have done something to Dana's place." His gaze roamed over the revolver and the nylon cord securing it.

"Fontenot? So your crazy notions about that bastard ain't so crazy, eh? Stay there, Cody. I'll be right over."

"Nope. Can't. Dana's out of town. Her answering machine says she'll be back tomorrow. I've got to check her house tonight. Dev? Can I count on you?"

"You know it, my man."

"Thanks." He flipped off the cell phone and walked over to look more closely at the .38 special. The cord had been run through the trigger guard and around the back of the chair, then fashioned to an intricate pulley mechanism attached to the doorknob.

He looked at the barrel of the gun, then at the door, then back at the gun.

Cody cursed as he took in the full implications of what he saw. "If you wanted me dead, I'd be dead, wouldn't I? You're playing with me."

Anger, harsh and swift, cut through him, then his knees went weak. "Dana," he whispered, refusing even to allow his brain to imagine what Fontenot might have done at her place. He reached into the pocket of his jacket and pulled out the tiny gold disk he'd found this morning on his car seat. He closed his fist around his ex-wife's earring.

"I swear to God, Fontenot," he whispered to the empty room. "If you hurt one hair on her head, I will hunt you down like the monster you are."

He glanced around his apartment, now a crime scene. Dev would take care of things here. Cody had to get to Dana's.

DANA MAXWELL SANK gratefully into the scented water. It was so hot her skin tingled. As she leaned her head back against the headrest molded into the fiberglass tub in her ultramodern apartment in Metairie, the stiffness began to seep out of her neck muscles. She rolled her head and groaned, flexing the aching tendons.

Why had she thought working in corporate law would be less stressful than the courtroom? Maybe it was less exciting, but spending an entire week in meetings with stodgy, old-guard businessmen who were stuck in the fifties, maybe even the forties, was not conducive to a good mood.

If she'd had to hear "honey" or "little lady" one more time, she thought she might have contemplated murder. Then, this afternoon, the senior partner had the gall to ask her to step outside while the "menfolks have us a confab that might not fall too sweetly on your pretty little ears."

Dana sank a little lower into the water. She'd stepped outside all right. She'd stepped out of the room and into her car and driven back to New Orleans, calling her office on the way and telling them she was sick, and wouldn't be in the next day, Friday.

She cringed. She'd walked out on an important meeting. She'd lied to her boss about being sick. Was there anything *else* she could think of to do to jeopardize her job?

Bennett was the biggest client her boss had ever assigned to her. Today was Thursday and she was supposed to have that new contract signed by Friday. What would Mr. Fraser do?

Over the weekend, she'd have to come up with a plausible excuse for walking out on Irwin, Borne and Howe's third-biggest corporate clients.

Are We Boring and How was the name Cody had given the law firm. She smiled involuntarily at the thought. He hadn't tried to stop her from quitting the public defender's office and moving to corporate law, but he'd looked at her in that way he had and said that being bored to death was a horrible way to go.

Dana frowned at the direction her thoughts were taking. Why was she thinking about that? She didn't want to go back there.

Ugh. She gave a mock shudder. *No way.* She'd had enough of long hours and hopeless cases to last her a lifetime.

And talk about tired. On countless nights, she had dragged in after nine or ten, dead on her feet, only to have to turn around and go back to work early the next morning.

Dana stretched her stiff neck muscles, thinking longingly of the big old claw-foot tub in Cody's French Quarter apartment. Now, *that* tub was made for relaxing. She would fill it up, sink down until the water lapped at her nape like fingers teasing, massaging. The smile kept tugging at her lips. How many times had Cody run her a bath and crouched behind the tub to massage her neck? She closed her eyes, almost able to feel his fingers kneading, rubbing, coaxing out the stiffness as he whispered risqué suggestions in her ear.

Then his touch would lighten as her muscles relaxed, and he'd pick up the soap and run it over her shoulders, across her collarbone and down, until her breasts and belly were slick with suds and his teasing fingers were doing things with the soap that Procter & Gamble never dreamed of.

"Damn it, Cody, get out of my head," Dana muttered, splashing water as she sat up. It was all his fault. If he hadn't called earlier in the week, his voice sounding oddly serious on her answering machine, she wouldn't be fighting off these memories that should have had no meaning for her anymore.

She blinked away a stinging sensation behind her eyelids and pushed thoughts of Cody out of her brain.

How could a man be so easy to love and so impossible to live with?

She picked up the soap and began washing her shoulders and arms briskly, thinking longingly of a glass of wine, a new book and soft white sheets.

Tomorrow, she would ignore her conscience and drive up to the lake. She could actually have a mini-vacation, the first one she'd taken since…well, in a long time. A weekend at the converted fishing shack on Lake Pontchartrain that belonged to her grandfather's best friend was just what she needed. Then she could relax and think up answers to the questions her boss would fire at her on Monday.

She'd made up her mind on the way home today. She'd even written it in her day planner.

Friday: buy junk food, buy two romance novels, spend weekend alone at the lake house, reading and eating.

She'd leave all her messages unanswered, her mail unpicked up, and just go. Maybe on Sunday, she'd pull up some weeds and replant the bulbs she'd planted four years ago, the last time she and Cody had gone up there together, right before that awful night when Cody had nearly died.

Dana shook her head angrily. She was not going to let the memories get to her this weekend. It had been four years. She was doing fine. Just fine.

A muffled thump echoed through the apartment. She jumped, then froze, but she heard nothing else. It was probably the neighbor's dog knocking over her trash can again. She sank back into the water.

The bathroom door swung open slowly.

Her heart slammed into her chest. She couldn't scream, couldn't even get a breath. Her gaze darted quickly around the room but there was nothing she could use as a weapon. Her fingers clutched the wet soap as the door creaked and the sound of labored breathing reached her ears.

A scuffed brown loafer appeared and an irritatingly familiar voice said, ''What the hell are you doing here?''

''Damn it, Cody!'' The soap slipped from her fingers and plopped into the water. She forced a huge gulping breath into her lungs and sank even lower, trying in vain to spread the washcloth over her breasts. ''You scared the daylights out of me.''

Relief that it was just Cody set her heat-loosened muscles to quivering as a wave of anger washed over her. Then his words sank in.

Her face burned. ''What do you mean what am I doing here? I live here. The question is what are you doing here? Get out of my bathroom. How did you get in?''

Cody grinned stiffly and held up a bank card. ''Accepted in thousands of locations worldwide.''

''Somehow I never pictured you carrying a gold card,'' she muttered, looking him over. There was something wrong. His smart-mouthed remark hadn't sounded quite biting enough. His voice had a hollow ring and his grin was crooked and meager.

His jeans were brown with dust. An angry red scratch marred his cheek and a bruise discolored his forehead. He leaned against the bathroom door trying to look insolent and nonchalant, but he was pale as a ghost and his jaw was clenched tight.

Still, that didn't keep his gaze from roaming over her with a hunger she could feel along every wet, trembling inch of her body. It affected her just like it always had. Even if her mind was determined not to get caught up in painful memories, her body had no such compunction. A wave of remembered desire streaked through her, making her legs feel like jelly and her breasts tighten, intensifying her anger.

She tried to make the washcloth cover more, and drew up one leg in an attempt to cover her nakedness. "Get out of here," she snapped. "Hand me my robe."

He shook his head slightly and winced. "Nice to see you, too," he muttered dryly, then grabbed her robe and tossed it toward the tub.

She caught it just in time to keep it from falling into the water. "Get out of here, Cody." She stood, holding the robe in front of her.

He complied without comment.

When she came out of the bathroom, he was right by the door, so she had to squeeze past him. She marched into the living room in her bare feet and started to open the blinds. "Would you please tell me why you—"

"Don't," he interrupted in an oddly quiet but compelling voice.

She shrugged and left the blinds closed, then turned to peer at him in the darkness. He looked tired and bedraggled. His trademark leather jacket wasn't sitting quite as carelessly on his wide shoulders. The collar wasn't turned rakishly up. His posture wasn't the insolent hip-cocked leaning that always sent a shiver of desire through her. He looked...exhausted. Something was wrong.

Dana forced her thoughts away from how her ex-husband looked. She reminded herself that he was here because he'd broken into her apartment. "I have a perfectly good doorbell. Would you please tell me why you felt you had to break in?"

"I thought you were still gone," he said. "How

many times have I told you not to put that kind of information on your…answering machine? The whole city of New Orleans doesn't…need to know you'll be out of town until Friday. You might as well take out an ad—'I'm gone. Please…steal me blind.'''

She ignored the strain in his voice. ''Oh, I see. You only broke in because you thought I was gone? You've turned to burglary now, I guess. The police force isn't dangerous enough for you.'' She switched on the lamp and pulled her robe tighter around her.

Her fingers touched something sticky on the terry cloth. She looked down. Dark red streaked the front of her robe, where she'd brushed by Cody, and stained her fingers. Blood. It was blood. Slowly, reluctantly, her brain wrapped itself around the thought. Her throat closed. She looked at Cody, a sickening dread overriding her anger.

His left arm hung uselessly at his side, and in the lamplight, she saw what she hadn't noticed before. Blood dripped slowly onto the floor.

''Oh, Cody, you're bleeding. What have you done now?'' she moaned, mesmerized and horrified by the dark drops that trickled down his motionless fingers to fall onto the polished wood.

He shrugged and tried to grin, but a grimace of pain crossed his face. His eyes closed and his legs buckled and he slid down the wall.

Through lips white with pain, he muttered, ''Dana, don't be mad. I'll leave.''

Déjà vu surrounded her in shades of slowly dripping red, spinning her head crazily. ''You obviously can't leave. You can't even—'' her voice caught on a sob ''—stand up.'' She hated her accusing, bitter tone, but she couldn't help it. She'd been here, done this, and she didn't want the T-shirt.

"Look at you. Damn it, Cody...." He hadn't changed—although that was no surprise. He'd never changed and he never would. He would always step right into danger's path. He would always be the same cocky, brash kid she'd fallen in love with at first sight.

They'd only dated a few weeks before Cody had talked her into getting married. She'd been in law school, and he'd just joined the New Orleans Police Department. But that was a long time ago. Now their marriage was over, and he had no right to come into her house, bleeding and hurt. He had no right to make her start worrying about him again. She opened her mouth to say so, but his head lolled to one side and his body slumped.

"Oh, God." She stared at her ex-husband, passed out on the floor. She kneeled down and pushed his silky hair out of the way to feel his forehead. "Cody, wake up! What do I do?"

He opened his eyes and looked a little to the left of her head. "Whoa," he whispered. "There's two of you, Dana. Wow, twice as much to love."

Something deep inside her ached with loss and sorrow. *No. Please don't use the word* love. *I can't stand it.* She concentrated on helping him.

"Where are you hurt? What happened?" She stood up and pulled on his unbloodied arm, trying vainly to master the queasy fear that was stealing her breath. Cody was hurt. *Again.* "Can you stand up?"

He looked at his left hand, covered in blood. "Look. I'm bleeding on your floor. I'm sorry, Dana, I know how much you hate a mess." His voice was faintly slurred. He wiped his fingers on his jeans, streaking the dusty fabric with thick black blood and shearing what was left of Dana's breath from her lungs.

Her gaze followed the path of his hand. *Blood. Cody's blood.* ''Cody, shut up. Talk to me.''

Cody laughed weakly. ''Pick one, *chère.*''

''How bad are you hurt? Should I call a doctor?''

''No!'' He pulled himself upright with a huge effort. ''Please, Dana. No doctor. It's not that bad. Just a flesh wound. Damn,'' he whispered, leaning back against the wall, his face turning paler, if that was possible. His forehead furrowed and more lines appeared on his face. He looked as though he was in agony.

Dana's heart pounded so loudly the echoes seemed to reverberate around her. Cody was in trouble. It was the same old story, the same old Cody, and Dana felt the same old terror squeezing her chest.

Not again. I can't do it again.

Because she couldn't think of anything else to do, she grabbed his good arm and draped it around her shoulders. ''Damn it, Cody, when are you going to figure out you're not immortal? When are you going to realize that those bullets are real? This isn't cops and robbers. That's not make-believe blood.'' She stopped herself with an effort. Her voice was beginning to sound hysterical.

''When are you going to...remember my name is not 'Damn it, Cody.'''

She sniffed in exasperation. ''Come on. We've got to stop that bleeding.''

''I know. Messing up your floor.'' Cody was mumbling and leaning heavily on her. He was almost out again.

She glanced at the tiny bathroom, then dismissed it as too small. Instead, she turned him toward the bedroom. "Wait a minute. Can you stand, just for a second?" She peeled his arm from around her shoulder and jerked her new Battenberg lace bedspread off the bed.

Cody made a short, derisive sound and Dana's face burned. "It's brand new...." She stopped, embarrassed. He was bleeding to death and she was worried about a bedspread.

"Don't worry, *chère,* I understand. Hard to get that blood out...wouldn't want a stain. Wouldn't want a mess." His voice was fading, but she heard him.

She started to respond but Cody was losing his fight to stay upright. She caught him around the waist as he swayed.

"You still smell like roses," he said, his voice rumbling against her shoulder and his breath warm on her ear. "Al...always like roses."

And you smell like danger, and trouble, and everything I lost. "Can you stand up long enough to get the jacket off?"

"Maybe," he said. But just as she reached for the collar to pull it off his shoulders, his knees buckled again and he crumpled onto the bed. "Then again...maybe not."

"Damn it, Cody, how can you joke at a time like this? You're bleeding and in trouble. Try to take it seriously, please. Turn over. I've got to get that jacket off." She pulled at the sleeve, and when it slid off, she saw where the blood was coming from. Her stomach turned upside down and she had to swallow against the queasy lump that began to form.

"Oh, God," she breathed as her stomach pitched. "Cody, you've been shot."

"You got that right," he whispered, then groaned

as she tugged on the torn sleeve of his sweatshirt. It was soaked with blood and stuck to his skin. There was an ugly black hole in the upper arm.

She looked at his back. Another hole marred the shoulder. "Is—is this the same b-bullet? How many times were you shot?"

"Just once," he gasped. "It went clean through. I heard it hit the wall behind me."

Dana moaned at the picture his words evoked. "It went through," she repeated doggedly. "That's good, I think. We need to get you to the emergency room."

"No." Cody shook his head against the pillow and grabbed her wrist with his good hand. "Just wrap it up, please."

She pulled away. "God, Cody. You're the most stubborn man I've ever known. You need stitches, and probably a tetanus shot, and a blood transfusion for all I know."

"No, I don't. Got a tetanus shot, last year, when I—never mind. All they'd do is...wrap it up. Please, Dana?"

"Fine," she grumbled, grabbing a pair of scissors from the sewing box under her dressing table. "What do I care, anyway? It's none of my business. I don't know why you even came here."

Her fingers shook and her mouth filled with acrid saliva as she cut the sleeve of his sweatshirt. Nausea burned in her throat. She swallowed hard, while a shudder ran up her spine.

It was just like before. Like all the times before. "You haven't changed a bit. It's just like the last time, and the time before that. How many times were you shot in the two years we were married? Three times? Four?''

Dana hadn't seen much blood in her life, and most of it was Cody's.

Chapter Two

Dana licked dry lips as she peeled fabric away from Cody's skin. It didn't matter if he'd been shot three times or thirty. It was too many. The last time had been a head wound. Then the blood had streaked his forehead and his cheek and had run down his neck to soak the collar of his shirt.

"And how many times did you go to the doctor? Once. And that wasn't even your idea. You were unconscious, for God's sake!"

She hadn't ever wanted to see his blood again. That was why she'd left him. It was the reason that, no matter how much she loved him, no matter how much it had hurt her, she'd had to leave. His job had always come first. Always had and always would.

"Dana, could you shut up and get on with it, please?"

She pushed the memories to the back of her mind and concentrated on getting the sweatshirt off without tearing open his wound. "Oh, Cody," she moaned.

His beautiful golden skin was torn and bloody. The holes in the sweatshirt matched the holes in his arm, right through the meaty part of his bicep. Blood oozed out of both wounds.

Dana stared in fascination as the present and the past rushed toward each other like runaway trains. She had to concentrate to keep them from colliding in her brain.

Cody. Wonderful, dangerous Cody. The only man she'd ever loved. Once she hadn't been able to imagine life without him.

Then, as she began to realize just what being the wife of a cop meant, the possibility of life without Cody became all too real. She'd already had more experience than she ever wanted of waiting at home for someone who never came back. She couldn't face that again, not even for Cody.

So she'd divorced him. He wasn't her problem anymore, hadn't been for four years.

She kept on talking, more in an effort to ground herself in the present than because she actually had anything to say. "How many times can it happen, Cody? How are you always in the middle of the danger? Why does it always have to be you?"

He didn't answer, just lay there, his sweat staining her new pillowcases, his eyes squeezed shut and a grimace of pain marring his even features.

She pressed her lips together and stood, holding out her bloodstained hands like a surgeon as she backed out of the room. "I think I still have some gauze pads and peroxide from the last time," she muttered as she walked into the bathroom, reached for the faucets and ran cold, clean water over her hands, watching in bitter fascination as Cody's blood ran down the drain.

She dug around in the bathroom cabinet until she found the supplies, and brought them and a wet washcloth back into the bedroom.

Even in the middle of this latest crisis with Cody,

the sight of him lying on her bed caught her off guard. She stopped dead still in the doorway. For a split second, the years vanished, and she and Cody were together and in love. Dana was shocked at the spear of desire that streaked through her. She winced and shut her eyes briefly.

Cody opened his eyes to a slit and gazed suspiciously at the bottle of peroxide. "You brought that stuff with you when you moved out? That means it's four years old? You sure it's still good?"

Dana straightened. His words reminded her of why he was here. "I'm sure it's okay. I've kept it capped. Remember, the hospital gave it to me when I brought you home."

"I remember."

The bitterness in his voice surprised her. She glanced at his face, but he'd closed his eyes and his breathing was ragged. She sat down beside him on the bed.

"We were married two years and you were shot two times. It's like you're some kind of a bullet magnet."

Cody lay on his side, his mouth set, his jaw clenched, the tendons in his neck standing out. There were lines around his eyes, deep lines, lines that hadn't been there four years ago. Her fingers twitched to smooth them out. A strange regret raised a lump in her throat.

He licked his lips. "I'll tell them to quit picking on me, okay? To shoot somebody else for a change," he said hoarsely. "I'll tell them you said so. But could you shut up for a minute and give me some water and maybe an aspirin?" Beads of sweat gathered on his forehead and ran down his face. "I'm hurting a little."

The lump in her throat swelled and tears stung her

eyes. *Damn it, Cody. Don't make me feel sorry for you. I will not cry for you!*

She tried to steel herself against his pain. It had always scared her to death how vulnerable, how fragile he looked when he was hurt. Usually he was so strong, so competent, so capable. He'd always been bigger than life to her. His tall, lean body had always seemed invulnerable.

She'd trusted him, admired him, loved him with all her heart. She'd always loved to watch him move. He moved so fast, so gracefully for a tall man, handling himself like a dancer or a predatory cat, his energy and strength barely constrained inside his golden skin. But when he was hurt, like now, he looked smaller, human, breakable.

Dana forced herself to stop thinking and just act. She inspected his wounds and saw that blood still oozed down onto the remains of the sweatshirt. She poured peroxide onto the raw flesh. The liquid foamed and sizzled and Cody sucked in a long, hissing breath.

"Hey…" he groaned raggedly.

"I've got to clean it." Her voice sounded harsher than she'd intended, but she had to do something to stop the memories. She didn't want to be here doing this for this man who lived his life so close to death it had almost driven her insane. It *had* driven her away. *Why couldn't you love me enough to stay safe?*

Cody opened his eyes and looked at her. "I know. Sorry," he said, and smiled.

Oh, Cody. His smile stole her breath. It was still as angelic as it had always been. Her heart hurt to see him so pale and gaunt, smiling at her and apologizing.

The intervening years hadn't really made that much difference in him physically. He'd gotten harder, if that was possible, maybe leaner. Where before he'd been a handsome, cocky young man, now he was more mature, more solidly male, and even more handsome. The lines in his face added character.

His hair, damp and matted, was still honey-brown and soft as a baby's. His face was streaked with sweat, the skin drawn tight over the bones, but his eyes were the same electric blue, with thick brown lashes that were obscene on a man. Right now, the blue eyes seemed filled with pain and regret and something else she couldn't identify.

His gaze slid downward, and she felt it, like fingers, touching her neck, her collarbone, the hastily pulled-together edges of her bathrobe.

"Sorry I interrupted your bath," he whispered. "You always hated that."

"Ha," she sniffed. "I never got to finish a bath the whole time we were married." As soon as she said the words, she regretted them.

His eyes lit with amusement, and Dana knew with the intimate knowledge of two years of marriage what he was thinking. The same thing she was. They both remembered how many of her baths had ended with damp, tangled sheets and shared laughter. Dana felt the liquid heat that had always burned through her at his touch. She saw the spark of it in his eyes.

Embarrassed by her thoughts and the knowledge that he was reading them, she mangled a strip of tape as she applied it, then impatiently ripped it off. He jerked and grimaced. "Ouch. What are you trying to do, kill me?"

"I don't have to. You're doing a fine job of it by yourself," she retorted. "Now, shut up." Her mouth tight, she finished taping up his wounds. She cut the ruined sweatshirt off and slid his jacket out from under him, working doggedly, trying to ignore his labored breaths and the occasional quiet grunts when she hurt him.

"How did you get shot this time?" she asked in spite of herself. If she could take back the question, she would have. She didn't want to know. She didn't want to own the knowledge of this latest proof of Cody's mortality.

"You wouldn't believe me if I told you," he said softly, his words slurring.

She breathed a sigh of relief, ignoring the tiny inner voice that speculated on how bad the answer must be if he didn't want her to know. She didn't need another life-size image for her mental scrapbook—Cody being shot, Cody falling, Cody lying still and pale on the ground.

She finally finished dressing his wounds, thankful when his torn flesh was covered. It scared her to realize how fragile he was, merely human under his skin, no matter how invulnerable he appeared. Biting her lower lip, she pushed the thoughts out of her head. It wasn't her problem anymore if he got himself shot once a year or once a month.

"Dana?" he whispered.

"What, Cody?" she asked curtly as she gathered up the towels and washcloths and his jacket. She turned back toward the bed. "Well?"

"Thanks."

The word cut through her like a knife. Her suddenly nerveless fingers almost lost their grip on his clothes. "Don't thank me. Don't try to play on my sympathy. Why did you come here? Why would you think I'd want to help you? Damn it, Cody, why?"

His eyes opened and he looked up at her, a small smile quirking his mouth. "I told you. I didn't think you were here. My apartment wasn't—safe. Besides, you're the one person I know I can trust, no matter what."

"No!" she shouted, throwing the clothes toward the bathroom. "Don't say that, Cody. Don't try to make me responsible. You've got the entire New Orleans Police Department to watch out for you. You didn't have to come running to me. I am *not* going to patch you up and send you back out there. I can't do it. I'm where I want to be. I'm finally over...everything, and I won't let you turn my life all upside down again."

A flicker of darkness clouded his eyes, but his voice was light, if a bit hollow, when he replied. "Don't worry. I'll be out of here tomorrow, okay?" He closed his eyes, his lashes resting like fuzzy caterpillars on his scratched cheek. He'd fallen asleep or passed out.

Dana reached out a trembling hand and pushed his silky hair back from his forehead. Without her conscious consent, her thumb traced the faint lines, less prominent now that he was asleep. She deliberately kept her eyes off his naked chest and abdomen, trying not to remember his delicious planes and curves. She tried not to drink in the sight of him, golden and familiar, in her bed. Deliberately, she focused on his shoulder, but that only made her ache with compassion and wince with empathic understanding of how badly he was going to hurt when he woke up.

She gritted her teeth. He didn't deserve her compassion or her empathy. He was her ex-husband. And the operative part of that word was "ex."

She'd filed for divorce because she hadn't had the strength to patch up his wounds again. *His or her own.*

He'd loved her, she'd never doubted that. Just not enough. He'd loved the danger more. She'd thought she could handle being a cop's wife. But Cody could never be just a cop. He had to go for the dangerous cases. He craved the excitement. And it was going to get him killed. It had already left its scars on both of them.

He had physical, external scars. But her scars were just as deep, just as permanent. On that awful night four years ago, while she'd waited to hear whether her husband would live or die, she had miscarried the baby they'd both wanted so badly. It had been the last link that had bound her to him. So as soon as she was sure he would be okay, she'd filed for divorce, because she couldn't bear losing anyone else.

"I just couldn't do it," she whispered, her fingers still lingering on the tightly drawn skin over his cheekbones. "I couldn't face years of that. Not again. Sitting at home, afraid that this might be the night you didn't make it." *Just like my father.*

She touched his mouth, the little lines that laughter had put there. "But, oh God, it was hard. You'll never know how hard it was to leave you. I miss your laughter." She shook her head. She must really be upset, to be talking to herself like this. She didn't miss the danger, she reminded herself sternly, looking down at her terry-cloth robe, where the blood was already drying. The danger more than canceled out the fun.

She was content now...she was safe. She was no longer in love with Cody...not at all. She certainly was not responsible for him anymore. She'd shed that responsibility along with her wedding ring four years ago.

Sighing, she lay down next to him, her eyes still

tracing his beloved features, trying not to notice the paleness in his face, trying not to hear his ragged breathing, trying desperately and without success not to care what happened to him.

When he woke up, he'd have to leave.

FONTENOT SAT UP into the night, soldering, wiring, testing, until he was satisfied with his latest creation. Finally, he stood, stretching cramped muscles, and walked around it, surveying it critically.

His face creased in a slow smile. Perfect. Naturally. He held up the bottle of spring water, toasting himself, then took a sip. No alcohol, nothing but natural substances went into his body. Chemicals interfered with brain function, and nothing was going to interfere with his perfect plan. His perfect revenge.

Nothing and nobody.

He stared out the window, thinking about the booby trap he'd rigged at Maxwell's apartment. His lip curled in disdain. Maxwell wasn't as smart, or as quick, as he'd given him credit for being.

He'd heard the sharp retort of the gun, at the very second he'd predicted. Then a few minutes later Maxwell had come rushing out and headed for his car. But Fontenot had overestimated the detective. He'd timed the trigger mechanism perfectly, to a reaction time designed for a man in Maxwell's physical condition. But the stupid man had been too slow, so the bullet, which should have harmlessly hit the wall behind him, had instead caught him in the shoulder.

He had to give Maxwell credit, though. Even with his shoulder bleeding, and his face pale with pain and fear, he'd still cranked up his car and headed for Metairie, for his ex-wife's house, just like Fontenot had known he would.

Fontenot chuckled. *Just wait, Maxwell. I'm not through with you yet. Before I'm done you'll suffer for every minute I spent in prison. You'll wish you were dead.*

He finished his water and went back to his creation, considering the best way to set it up for installation. He had to be able to set it up in five minutes, and not one second more.

The sweet throb of anticipation began within him. This would be even better than the booby-trapped gun. He took a long, shuddering breath and went back to work.

Chapter Three

Cody was in hell. He was doing his best to fight his way out, but he wasn't having much luck, because Satan had his pitchfork rammed through Cody's shoulder, and he wouldn't let go. Cody jerked against the devil's grip.

Damn, that hurt! He tried to turn around and attack but for some reason, he couldn't move. He took a long breath, preparing to try again, but mingled in with the sulfur and brimstone in the air was the delicate scent of roses.

"Ahh!" Cody jerked awake. His shoulder felt as if it was still in hell, but as he came to consciousness, he remembered where he was. He was at Dana's. How had he gotten all the way out here to Metairie?

His head cleared slowly, and he remembered the rest of it. The booby trap at his apartment. The pain. The fear that Fontenot had rigged a similar trap for Dana, and his relief when he'd found nothing wrong. Then his surprise when he'd discovered her in the bathtub. She had changed her plans. Dana *never* changed her plans.

He sniffed the air again. *Roses.* Without raising his head, he opened his eyes. He was in her bedroom, in her bed, and she was lying next to him. He looked at her across the hills and valleys of white cotton sheets. She was asleep, on top of the covers, still wrapped in the bloodstained terry-cloth robe. Her hands were clenched into fists and curled against her breast.

It was how she'd slept during the last few disastrous months of their marriage, all scrunched up, like she was sleeping as fast and as hard as she could, like sleeping was just another chore, along with taking out the garbage, or paying the bills, or putting up with him.

He frowned. She'd always hated his job. Sometimes he didn't blame her. Sometimes he hated it, too, like last night when he'd opened his apartment door and realized a split second too late what Fontenot had done.

The quiet click of the hammer should have been enough warning. But it wasn't. He was lucky the bullet had only torn through the flesh of his upper arm. If he'd been a split second slower, it would have caught him square in the chest. He snorted.

That's what Dana would say. Four years ago he'd have responded by saying that a split second faster and it would have missed him. But it hadn't missed him, and Cody knew why. He'd been preoccupied with worry for his ex-wife.

The day the jury returned the verdict that sent Fontenot to prison, the madman had smiled serenely at Cody and promised he'd be back, his gaze resting briefly but meaningfully on Dana.

Cody got the message, and Fontenot knew it.

Now Fontenot was free because of an overcrowded prison system and slick lawyers, and Cody still remembered that smile and his meaningful look. Cody had no doubt that Fontenot would make good on his threat. He had no doubt Dana was in danger.

She stirred and murmured softly, and memories of the two of them crowded thoughts of Fontenot out of Cody's brain. As he watched, she moved a little closer, and briefly, he saw the young, serious law student he'd fallen in love with all those years ago. She appeared carefree and relaxed, without that tiny double line between her eyebrows, without the ever-so-slightly turned-down mouth that made her look older than she was.

He lay there, ignoring his aching shoulder, and watched her sleep. The faint lines around her eyes smoothed out, and a hint of a smile curved her mouth.

God, she was gorgeous. His mouth turned up. She'd always objected when he said that. She never got over the idea that he was just teasing her. She'd never quite believed how much he loved her olive-green eyes, the dark blond wavy hair she complained about, even the crooked front tooth that made her look impish when she grinned.

With an effort, he moved his injured arm and curled his fingers loosely around hers. The tension in her clenched fist made his chest ache. She'd always been too serious. Always worried about the damnedest things. She obviously hadn't changed much, he thought wryly.

He rubbed his thumb across her knuckles, savored the softness of her skin against his. He loved to touch her. She was like silk over steel, her skin as soft as an angel's. But it was the steel that fascinated him. He admired her determination, her certainty. She never had doubts, never made mistakes.

Except for him. He was her only mistake, and he

knew how much she regretted making it. He'd come into her comfortable little world and dared to disrupt it. She was safety and stability and he was danger.

He'd always wanted to be a cop. Dana knew that before she'd married him. But when it came down to the reality of it, she hadn't been able to live with the danger and uncertainty that was a part of him.

But while it was good, it was very, very good. He reached to push a hair away from her cheek, forgetting his injured arm.

"Ouch!" he growled, and cursed.

Dana stirred, turning toward him. She opened her eyes, and when her green gaze met his, it was like old times. Her mouth softened and she almost smiled. "Morning, tough guy."

"Morning, *chère*," he said, his voice hoarse with emotion.

Her eyes widened and she stiffened, although how she could have gotten any more tense was beyond his comprehension. She'd remembered why he was here, and she wasn't having any of his New Orleans charm. He knew because the two little frown lines had reappeared in her forehead. She sat up.

"Oh. I forgot you were…how is your shoulder?" she asked, pushing her hair out of her eyes. The silky blond strands caught around her fingers, and she winced as she disentangled them, scattering pins as the waves tumbled around her face and neck.

Cody didn't move, partly because it hurt less when he stayed still, and partly because Dana's robe had come loose and he could see about eighty percent of one delicately veined breast. His pulse sped up as he remembered the feel of her small, perfect breasts under his palms.

Dana frowned and followed his gaze. "Humph. Grow up, Cody."

"Why?" he muttered. "So I can be as grumpy and stodgy as you?"

She glared at him. "No, so you can get a real job and quit playing cops and robbers." She pulled her robe together and got up, then looked down at the brown streaks on the terry cloth as if she'd never seen them before. Her face grew white and she clenched her jaw.

She looked up at him, accusation and pain in her olive-green eyes. "Go away, Cody," she said tonelessly, holding up one hand, palm out. "Just...go away."

She left the room and Cody turned gingerly onto his back, staring up at the ceiling. Nothing had changed. She still blamed him. Of course, he knew how she felt, because he blamed himself.

He'd never had a chance to talk to her after he'd gotten out of the hospital. Not really talk. She'd done an excellent job of avoiding him, even while they were still living together. Then, once he'd recuperated enough to go back to work, she'd moved out, and their communications had been through their lawyers.

He'd tried over and over to tell her how sorry he was. He'd wanted to grab her and hold her and grieve with her over the baby they'd lost. He'd have promised her anything just to wipe the sadness from her eyes. He'd have sworn to her that he'd get out of police work, that he'd sack groceries if she'd just come back to him, but he never got the chance.

She left him.

So he'd thrown himself even deeper into his job. But it was never quite the same out there without her to come home to. He hadn't realized how much he depended on her to be there, until she was gone.

There was still the satisfaction of putting a criminal behind bars, but without Dana to celebrate with him, it didn't mean as much. Her admiration for his devotion to his job had been lost somewhere along the way, and with it had gone a lot of his reason for wanting to do a good job.

Slowly, gingerly, he got out of bed and made his way into the kitchen. Dana had changed into jeans and a T-shirt and was drinking coffee from his favorite mug, the one with the chipped rim. He lowered himself carefully into a chair.

"I thought you couldn't find my mug," he remarked, faintly accusing. "It disappeared when you moved out." He was a little surprised that she'd kept it.

Dana's face burned and her fingers tensed around the rough surface of the pottery mug. "I couldn't. It was in the bottom of a box."

"That was my favorite mug."

"It's not your mug, it's my mug. I made it."

"I know," he said, smiling. "It never sat evenly. I spilled my coffee at least once a week because it wobbled."

Dana couldn't look at him, and she couldn't unwrap her fingers from the mug. She *had* made it for him. It was the only thing she made during that whole ceramics class that hadn't cracked in the kiln. He'd always claimed it was his favorite. Why, she had no idea.

With a supreme effort, she managed to speak. "If you want it, you can take it with you when you *leave*."

Cody shook his head and clenched his jaw against

the throbbing ache in his shoulder. He hadn't missed her emphasis on the word *leave.* "Got any aspirin?"

She nodded without looking at him and stood up. As she got the tablets and a glass of water and a mug of coffee for him, he looked around the kitchen, wondering what Fontenot had done to her apartment while she was out of town.

"Sit down, Dana," he said as he took the coffee from her unsteady fingers. "We need to talk."

"There is absolutely nothing to say," she said, but she sat down and picked up the chipped mug and wrapped her fingers around it again.

Cody watched as she realized what she'd done and put it down abruptly. It wobbled slowly and noisily on the table until he stopped it with his fingers.

It was funny how the oddest things took on meaning between two people. He loved the mug because she'd made it. He let it go. It wobbled again until he stopped it. If it had been perfect, it wouldn't be nearly as precious.

"I tried to call you Tuesday," he said, letting his fingers trace the whorls on the mug's surface. Why had she kept it? he wondered. It hadn't meant anything to her.

"I know. I picked up my messages."

"Why did you come back last night? Your answering machine said you'd be gone until today."

"I couldn't take Big Daddy and his good old boys talking at me like I was a simpering southern belle."

Cody looked up. "Big Daddy?"

Dana shrugged and her mouth turned up. She reached out and took the mug. "The ultraimportant client I met with in Baton Rouge. You know the type. He owns a chain of hardware stores there. He wants to expand to New Orleans and I was drawing up the contracts. He was insulting, so I walked out.''

Cody laughed. ''You walked out? Dana Maxwell walked out on a meeting with clients? I do believe hell has frozen over again. Call Don Henley and tell him to do another album.''

Dana banged the mug down on the table. His easy, intimate humor invaded places inside her she didn't want exposed. The two of them, sitting together drinking coffee, reminded her of lazy Sunday mornings and kisses flavored with café au lait, of her trying to study, while he....

''I can't do this. I can't sit here and have an idle, ordinary conversation with you. We're not old friends sharing a cup of coffee and memories. I want you out of here,'' she groused, lifting her head.

The laughter faded from his eyes and their blue brightness dulled to a gunmetal gray. ''Dana, there's something you need to know. Did you find anything out of place when you got back? Anything unusual?''

She heard a strange note in his voice. The frown on his face intensified her apprehension. Cody was worried about something, and that wasn't like him. She shook her head. ''Nothing except an ex-husband breaking in and bleeding all over everything.''

Cody reached his right hand awkwardly into his left jeans pocket and pulled something out. The movement obviously caused him pain, and she ached to see him hurt. She blinked fiercely, reminding herself his pain was no longer her concern.

But she had trouble dragging her gaze away from his bare chest with its faint dusting of honey-brown hair, and his broad shoulders, still streaked with dried blood.

He held up a small golden disk.

"What's that? Is that mine?" She reached out and took it from his fingers. It was one of the gold coin earrings he'd given her on their first anniversary. They had cost way too much, but she loved them. She'd worn them almost every day until their divorce. Since then they'd lain in her jewelry box under her bed.

She stared at it. "What are you doing with my earring?"

He covered her hand with his, wrapping her fingers around the disk. "*Chère,* look at me."

Reluctantly she raised her head. Something was very wrong. A frisson of fear slithered up her spine.

"This earring was on the seat of my car two mornings ago. I almost didn't see it."

She tugged against his grip, but he wouldn't let go. The post of the earring dug into her palm. "Stop it, Cody. It's obviously not my earring, then, because mine is in my jewelry box. You're just trying to scare me."

"It is yours. Go check."

"I'm not going to check. If it's mine then you got it out of my jewelry box this morning. Why are you doing this to me?"

Cody shook his head, his eyes dark and cloudy. She didn't want to look into them, didn't want to see the pain and the fear deep in those eyes that had so often sparked with laughter, but she couldn't pull her gaze away.

"Fontenot is out of prison."

She froze. "F-Fontenot?"

He nodded grimly.

"The man who shot you," she said. "How—how can he be out?"

"Good behavior, and good lawyers."

Dana closed her eyes. "He put a bullet in your head. He almost killed you. They can't let him out."

"Dana, listen to me. Fontenot swore he'd make me pay for putting him away. 'I shot you this time, but there are things that hurt more than a gunshot, Maxwell,' he said." Cody's blue eyes burned into hers.

She jerked her hand away and stood abruptly. "I don't care, Cody," she lied. She remembered Fontenot. Too well. She'd been with the public defender's office, but as the wife of the detective who'd been shot, she was barred from participating in the case.

She'd already filed for divorce by the time Fontenot came to trial, and she'd tried to stay away from the courtroom, but she'd had to hear the verdict with her own ears. She had to be there, to be sure they put that monster away.

"He looked at you when he said it." Cody stared at her. "And now, he's back. He got your earring out of this apartment without you even knowing he'd been here."

"That's ridiculous," she countered. "I'd know if anyone had been here."

Cody shrugged carefully. "Go check."

She could hardly catch her breath, the growing fear was sitting so heavily on her chest. "Why are you doing this?" she asked again, still unwilling to believe that Fontenot was out of prison and once again a danger to Cody. "I don't want to be in the middle of your blood feud with that madman."

"You don't have a choice. Fontenot isn't asking your permission. You are in the middle of it."

Old grief and pain ripped through her like a straight razor and her voice shook with passion and fury. "Because of you. You walked into that courtroom with your head still bandaged, so weak you had to lean on a cane, just so you could prove to the world that Cody Maxwell was tough enough to put him away.''

She took a shaky breath. "He almost killed you. *Your job* almost killed you. It did kill my baby. And I am never going through that pain again!''

She gasped at her own words. It was the first time she'd ever said it aloud, to him, and she saw the effect of her words etched in the new lines on his face.

An anguish too profound to bear washed over his features, draining the color from his face. But then, anger replaced the anguish, and he vaulted up from the chair and grabbed her arm with his good hand.

"*Our* baby," he ground out between clenched teeth, his face so close to hers she could feel the heat of his breath on her mouth, could see the darkness behind his blue eyes. "It was our baby, not just yours. I came home from the hospital to find out my wife was divorcing me and the baby we'd wanted so badly was never going to be born.''

He took a ragged breath and released her arm, pushing her away. "So don't talk to me about pain. Pain is something I know all about.''

He whirled and stalked out of the kitchen, his naked back and bare feet not detracting at all from his stiff, oddly dignified exit.

It was true. By the time he'd come home from the hospital, she might as well have already been gone. Then when she had moved out, he'd never questioned anything. He'd just gone along with whatever her lawyer wanted. At the time she'd thought he didn't care. She'd never even considered how he might be feeling.

No. She clenched her fists and squeezed her eyes

shut, determined not to cry. She could not let him get to her. She'd promised herself a long time ago she would never cry again, not for him, not even for herself. She'd already cried all her tears.

She stood in the middle of the kitchen until the stinging at the back of her eyes subsided. She realized she was still holding the mug—his mug. She set it down so hard she was afraid it might break, but it was tough.

She smiled grimly. Tougher than she was. The mug had made it through their two years of marriage with only a tiny chip in the rim. She hadn't fared as well. Her heart and soul had been scarred, and she wasn't sure those scars would ever go away.

She followed Cody into the bedroom and found him standing in the middle of the room, looking around. As she watched he went over to the bed and crouched down.

"What are you doing?"

"This is where you keep your jewelry case, isn't it?" he asked without looking up.

"Cody, do you mind? This is not a crime scene, it's my bedroom. Your shoulder is bleeding again. Aren't you going to go to the doctor?"

He stood and held the jewelry case out to her. She looked up to find his blue eyes regarding her with a mixture of impatience and triumph. "It is a crime scene, *chère*. Take a look. There's only one earring in there."

She jerked the box away from him. "Don't you want to preserve the fingerprints?" she asked acidly.

"Fontenot's too smart for that. You couldn't even tell he'd been in here, could you? You said there was nothing out of place."

Dana tried to remember walking into her apartment the day before. She'd been distracted, thinking about how she was going to tell her boss she'd just walked out on his biggest client. The apartment could have been turned inside out and she probably wouldn't have noticed.

"No..." she said tentatively. "No. I'm sure. I'd have noticed."

Cody looked meaningfully at the jewelry case, so she sighed and opened it. Nothing looked out of place, except that there was only one coin earring. She picked up her pearls and pushed aside a bracelet. The other earring wasn't there.

"I must have lost it," she said in a small voice.

Cody laughed. "You never lose anything. Remember the time I thought I'd lost my wedding band? You had put it where I always kept it. I didn't find it because I'd already looked there."

The grin slowly faded from his face. "That was early on, before I found out nothing ever gets lost around you. You won't allow it."

For some reason, Cody's words embarrassed her. He'd always made fun of her orderly ways. His teasing had been endearing once. Anger and embarrassment crowded into her breast, along with a peculiar longing for that long-ago time, before Cody's dogged determination to save the world alone had turned her neatly ordered life into chaos.

"Why are you so sure he got into my apartment? Nobody just waltzes into an apartment, finds a hidden jewelry case and takes one earring. That's ridiculous."

"It's not ridiculous if his purpose is to show me how close he can get to someone I—to you. You wore those earrings every day. You wore them in the courtroom. Fontenot doesn't miss anything. He saw them. He knew I'd understand the significance.''

''The significance. And just what is the significance, Detective?''

''The significance is that he can go anywhere. He can do anything. The man is psychotic, but he's brilliant. He could just as easily have been waiting for you here.''

''I don't want to...'' She turned away, frightened by the intensity of his gaze.

He caught her arm. ''Listen to me. Ever since they let him out of prison, things have been happening. Little things at first, but escalating.''

''Th-things?'' she stammered, against her will.

''A cup of coffee on my desk from Mintemans, my favorite place. And I didn't order it. Then my car was on empty one night when I got home, and full the next morning.''

''I don't...understand.'' She was lying, of course. She understood, too well. Cody had always maintained that Fontenot was diabolical. He'd been obsessed with putting the man away. Dana knew what Cody was telling her *shouldn't* make sense, but it did. It made frightening sense, because it meant that Cody was right about Fontenot. A horrible, shivery feeling skittered up her spine.

''Then, yesterday morning,'' Cody continued, ''I opened my car door, and this—'' he dangled the earring in front of her eyes ''—was on the driver's seat.''

''How...?'' She bit her lip. She did not want to know how he'd gotten shot, but she couldn't help herself. ''How did you get shot?''

For a split second, an unguarded look appeared in

his eyes. A look of fear. Dana's heart pounded. "Cody?"

He shook his head angrily. "I was...distracted."

"What do you mean?"

"Look, Dana. I guarantee you, you don't want to know."

"You're right, but I'm afraid I need to."

"I'm late. I've got to get out of here." He looked around the bedroom. "Is there an old sweatshirt of mine around here? Or a T-shirt?"

Dana started to press him for the answer, but her pounding heart was stealing her breath. He was right. She didn't want to know.

Reluctantly she went to her dresser and pulled out his police academy T-shirt, the one she slept in. She smoothed her palm over the soft material before she handed it to him. It was sad, in a ridiculously sentimental way, to give it up. His shirt had comforted her on many a lonely night. Somehow, she felt safe when she slept in it.

"My academy T-shirt. I thought I'd lost it. I should have known you'd still have it." He grinned at her as he shook it out, preparing to pull it on over his head. "Do you have anything else that belongs to me?"

Dana's face burned. "No," she snapped, a queer regret settling into her heart. When he left, taking his mug and his shirt with him, she wouldn't have anything that belonged to him. "Absolutely nothing. Aren't you ready to leave yet? I've got plans for this weekend."

"You've got plans for every moment of your life," Cody remarked dryly as he prepared to don the shirt.

She wanted to turn away. She didn't want to watch his lean muscles undulate as he pulled the T-shirt over his head. She certainly didn't want to see him wince as he lifted his wounded left arm. But somewhere along the way her will had gotten lost, so she stood helplessly, her eyes filled with the sight of the shirt molding his chest and abdomen.

With a grunt he finally got the shirt on and smoothed his hands down the front of it. She swallowed nervously. That T-shirt had clung to her breasts so many nights. Her own hands had smoothed the material across her belly, seeking comfort when she lay alone in bed.

His hands had once roamed over her like they now ran down his own body. No. Not exactly like this. This was a natural grooming gesture. He was just making sure the shirt was in place. His hands on her had been different—gentle but insistent, seeking, touching, teasing, and always, always strong.

She licked her lips and dragged her gaze away from the word *Academy* stretched across his chest.

"I'm going to check your apartment and take a look around outside."

"What?" she asked, distracted.

"I'm going to take a look around," he repeated. "What's the matter with you?"

She quickly turned away, pretending to look for something on the dresser. It wouldn't do for Cody to get a good look at her face right now. She was sure every thought, every emotion inside her was written in her expression.

"Fine. Fine. Just get out of here. And go to the doctor, if you can manage to find the time, what with saving the world and all. You're going to have an awful scar there if you don't."

"It'll go with the rest of them."

''God knows you've got enough.'' She glanced up at his mirrored image, regretting her words, but not able to stop them.

''You're a cold woman, Dana,'' he said, shaking his head, a touch of sadness marring his features.

She turned around and looked at the man who had once meant everything in the world to her, and wondered if he would ever know how wrong he was. ''I have to be. Otherwise I'd never stop hurting.''

Cody's eyes changed, darkened. He took a step toward her, but she backed away.

''Don't...'' she snapped, holding up a hand defensively. ''Just go.''

He shrugged, then winced when the movement hurt his shoulder. ''No problem, counselor,'' he said flatly. ''Send me a bill for services rendered.'' Then he turned on his heel and left.

Dana heard his shoes on the hardwood living room floor, then heard the front door open.

''Dana.''

She sighed in irritation and stepped through the hall to the living room. ''What?''

''Be careful, and call me if you notice anything strange. Anything, you understand? Fontenot isn't a man to mess with. I'll have a patrol car check the apartment.'' He turned to go then turned back one more time.

''What, Cody? What now?''

''Why don't you go over to Pensacola? Visit your sister. Get out of town for a day or two.''

''No. I told you, I have plans. Your life, your quarrels, your ex-cons full of revenge, don't have anything to do with me. I divorced you so I wouldn't be subjected to this. I have a life, a nice, quiet, boring life.

No danger, no heroics, no guns. I like it just fine.'' She folded her arms tightly and scrunched her shoulders, pulling in, away from his searing blue gaze.

She'd had more than she could take of Cody for one day—for a lifetime. His presence was opening wounds that hurt too much to be borne. ''Please go away and stay gone. I don't want to know when you get killed, thank you.''

A dark hurt shadowed his face briefly, then his mouth quirked in a wry smile. ''Oh, you're welcome, my dear ex-wife,'' he retorted. ''I guess I'd better change 'next of kin' in my official personnel file. But, Dana, just remember this. When I die, it'll be for something good, instead of dying of boredom, a day at a time, like you are.'' He slammed the door.

She stared at the door, peculiarly stung by his words. He held her sane, safe life in such contempt. Sometimes she couldn't figure out why he'd married her. Sometimes she wasn't sure why she'd married him.

Oh, she knew why she loved him...*had* loved him. Cody was easy to love. It had to do with the kind of man he was. He was an honorable man, a good man. A modern-day hero, a superman in jeans and a leather jacket. He truly believed that he could make a difference in the world. He'd been raised to be a cop, to spend his life keeping the world safe for others.

He believed in what he did. And therein lay the problem. Cody believed he was invincible. He believed the good guys always won. Moreover, he believed the good guys had a responsibility to the world.

Oh, Cody.

She closed her eyes and tried to feel relieved that he was gone, but all she could find inside her was a faint apprehension and a hollow sense of loss that had been there ever since she'd left him.

Chapter Four

Cody stomped down the steps. Dana was just as irritating as she'd ever been. Sometimes he wondered how he'd stood her rigid insistence on order for even two years. When they'd first met, she was so focused on getting her law degree, that he'd have to coax her to take an afternoon off. In her life, there was no room for spontaneity, no room for joy. Everything had to be just so, from the way the toilet paper rolled to the way they planned their vacations. The only time she let down her guard was when they made love.

The thought of her beneath him, her body covered with a sheen of sweat, her eyes filled with passion, her lips parted and swollen with kisses, hit him unawares. He almost stumbled on the last step.

''Hell,'' he muttered.

That part of it had always been good. Not just good...*great*. It always amazed him to watch the transformation he could bring about in her with just a touch.

Never, before or since, had a woman responded to him the way Dana had. Not that there had been many since, he thought wryly.

Somehow it wasn't the same anymore. The edge,

the wonder, wasn't there like it had been with Dana, so he'd found himself withdrawing, until he'd just about become a monk.

Cody shook his head to rid his brain of the distracting thoughts. What he needed to do was make sure Fontenot hadn't done something else, like booby-trap Dana's car. A sick fear gnawed at his insides. If anything happened to her…

He looked up and down the street, but there was nothing going on. It was Friday morning, and the only people stirring were businesswomen and men leaving for work.

He walked around her car, his eyes and his thoughts focused on noticing anything unusual, anything strange. He reluctantly dropped to the ground with a grunt, wincing as his shoulder throbbed with pain, and crawled underneath the car, looking for wires, or anything else that looked out of place. Nothing.

He dug his key, which he'd never given back to her, out of his jeans, and opened the car door, moving carefully, deliberately, listening and watching. The bastard wouldn't catch Cody Maxwell off guard again.

DANA REALIZED SHE'D BEEN staring at the apartment door ever since Cody had slammed it. She shook herself mentally. He was gone. He wasn't her problem anymore.

Then why did his hurt blue eyes still haunt her? Why did she feel like she'd just been treated to a brief moment in the sun, then had it snuffed out, leaving her alone and cold?

A shiver, like a cold rigor, slid up her spine. She pushed her maudlin thoughts away as she brushed her hair back from her face, and walked into the kitchen.

She could still drive up to the lake and spend a quiet couple of days. If she'd thought she needed a relaxing weekend before, now she was even more convinced. And it was obvious she wasn't going to get any rest around here with Cody playing cops and robbers.

She picked up the two coffee mugs to rinse them, then stared at her hands.

Cody's mug. Her fingers spasmed and she almost dropped it.

"Damn it, Cody," she muttered. "Why didn't you take it with you?"

She didn't want the rickety, chipped thing around. It was silly to have kept it all this time. She should have thrown it away years ago. She touched the little chipped place.

He'd made fun of it when she brought it home, but every time she'd tried to throw it away he'd insisted on keeping it.

"Once you get used to the way it wobbles," he'd told her, "it's a pretty nice mug."

She washed it carefully and dried it. *Stupid sentimentality!* Well, if Cody wanted the worthless thing she'd mail it to him or something. She set it beside her purse.

Looking at the clock, she hurried into the bedroom and threw some clothes into a travel bag. She didn't need anything fancy. She wasn't going to see a soul.

She stepped into the bathroom to get her makeup and nearly tripped over the pile of bloody clothes and towels. With a grimace of distaste, she picked up the towels. Underneath was Cody's leather jacket.

She picked it up half-reluctantly. The brown leather was creased and cracked, with scrapes and tears that

Dana was sure Cody could identify without missing a one. She knew several of them herself.

That huge scrape on one shoulder was where he'd been thrown out of a car going about sixty miles an hour. The tear in the cuff—

"Stop!" Dana yelled out loud. She wasn't going to get caught up in useless reminiscing. Without realizing it, she'd hugged the jacket to her breast. Deliberately catching it between finger and thumb like a dirty diaper, she went back into the kitchen.

There was no way Cody was going to insinuate himself back into her life. She didn't care if he'd gotten himself shot again. She didn't care if Fontenot was out of prison. Cody was wrong. It had nothing to do with her.

She avoided thinking about her earring.

She'd just take the cup and the jacket by his apartment on her way to the lake. That way he wouldn't have any reason to contact her.

After making sure her apartment was secure, the coffeepot was turned off and the timer was set to turn the lights on at dusk, Dana grabbed her travel bag and Cody's stuff and let herself out.

AFTER CODY HAD SATISFIED himself that he'd checked everything, he positioned his car at the corner of Dana's street, where he could see her front door, but she'd have a hard time seeing him, then he dialed Dev's cell phone.

"Dev, where y'at?"

"Trying to keep your sorry butt out of trouble, as usual. The captain's hot. I convinced him to let you alone last night, but you've got to make a statement."

"I know," Cody acknowledged. "I'll be there in

about an hour. Just as soon as Dana leaves for work. I want to be sure she's not followed.''

''Code, my man, this little booby trap here at your place is pretty slick.''

''I've been trying to tell you guys that Fontenot's a freaking genius. What'd you find?''

''What you'd expect. Nothing. It's a common .38 special. A street piece, no ID. We can run it through, but ten to one its pattern won't be in our files.''

Cody shook his head. ''Yeah, I know. And there are no fingerprints, and the cord was from my kitchen drawer.''

''You got it, my man.''

Cody flexed his shoulder and groaned. ''Look, Dev, I'm headed to the doctor as soon as I make sure Dana gets to work okay. Then I'll be on over. See if I can spot anything you guys missed.''

He held the phone away from his ear and grinned as Dev let loose with a string of colorful Cajun expletives that described in vivid detail what he thought about Cody finding anything he'd missed.

''Yeah, right. See you later.''

''Hey, buddy. The captain's got a place on his wall where he's planning to hang what's left of your ass after he chews it. I'd get over here sooner, rather than later.''

''On my way.'' Cody cut the connection, and briefly debated the advisability of taking the time to run to the doctor. His damn shoulder was throbbing like hell, and Dana was right, he probably did need stitches. He checked his watch. If Dana hadn't changed her habits, she'd be leaving for work in a few minutes. And he had to get to his apartment before the captain had a stroke.

He knew Fontenot was no fool. He wouldn't be within ten miles of Dana's apartment this morning, and he sure wouldn't go back to Cody's. He wouldn't take the risk of being caught at the scene of the crime.

Still, Cody didn't like the idea of Dana going anywhere without protection, even work. He picked up his cell phone again, to call and arrange for someone to keep an eye on her, when the door to her house opened.

Dana came out, a bundle of something in one arm and her purse and a travel bag slung over her other shoulder. What was she doing? It was obvious she wasn't going to work.

She hurried down the steps toward her car.

For an instant, Cody thought about waylaying her, but he decided he'd just follow her. She must have decided to go to her sister's after all. He'd just make sure she made it out of town safely, then he could get over to his apartment and see if there was anything he could spot that would connect Fontenot with his shooting.

As he shifted in the car seat, trying to find a position that didn't hurt his shoulder, he studied his ex-wife. She hadn't combed her hair or changed out of the faded jeans that hugged her shapely bottom so nicely. He squinted in the early morning sun. The bundle she carried was his leather jacket.

Cody raised an eyebrow. He couldn't believe he'd forgotten his jacket, but his mind had been on other things. He wondered what she was going to do with it. His mouth quirked in a mocking smile. Probably taking it to the cleaners. That would be just like her.

On her way out of town under threat from a dangerous criminal, Dana Charles Maxwell stopped at the

*cleaners to leave her ex-husband's leather jacket to
have the bloodstains removed.*

He pulled out behind her, keeping a safe distance
so she wouldn't spot him, and at the same time watching to be sure nobody else was following either of
them.

DANA PARKED IN FRONT of Cody's Rue Royal apartment, trying her best not to feel nostalgic. They'd lived
here together for the two years they'd been married.
As she dashed up the stairs, she wondered why he'd
kept it, after she moved out. Of course, he'd always
loved the old place. She had too, back then.

Early on, she'd rushed home every evening, anticipation quickening her heart, knowing Cody would be
there soon, knowing the evening would end in tender,
urgent lovemaking.

But after he'd been shot the first time, the anticipation began to turn to apprehension. Reality washed
with the color of Cody's blood, slammed her in the
face. Cody's job would always be like the ultimate
cops-and-robbers game to him. As she'd watched him
take more and more chances, she'd accepted that one
day he would end up dead.

So she'd begun to withdraw, and eventually, the
thrill of being with him, the love they'd shared wasn't
enough to make up for the old, familiar fear that
gnawed inside her every time he was late, or the phone
rang at odd hours of the night. She knew how awful
the silence of an endless night of waiting could be.
Would she have married him if she'd known she was
letting herself in for a replay of her early life, waiting
for her father to come home?

As she got to the third floor, she saw the yellow

Police Line tape across Cody's door and the uniformed officers milling around.

Her heart slammed into her throat, and her knees buckled. She had to grab the stair rail to keep from falling.

"Oh, no!" she breathed. *Cody!*

The man crouched in front of the door looked up. It was Dev, Devereaux Gautier, Cody's best friend and partner. His trademark scowl darkened his even features.

When he recognized her, the scowl deepened, and his black eyes flashed dangerously, then he stood and smiled, his white teeth shining behind the dark beard that shadowed his lean cheeks. "Dana! What are you doing here?" he said, his voice infused with false cheer. He walked toward her casually, but Dana wasn't fooled. Dev was trying to shield the scene with his body.

She grabbed his muscular arm. "Dev? What is it? What's happened? Where's Cody?"

He didn't answer, just put his hands on her shoulders and gently turned her away from the door. The grimness behind his false smile sent terror streaking through her.

"Dev, answer me! Is it Cody? Is he…dead?" Dana stared up into Dev's black eyes, praying he wouldn't say what she was deathly afraid of hearing, praying that Cody wasn't lying inside that police barricade dead. He'd been in her apartment less than an hour ago.

"Cody's okay. He's been shot, but you know the tough guy, there ain't no bullet that can bring him down. Bullets, they bounce off him." Dev tossed his head. His longer-than-regulation black hair immediately settled down on his forehead again.

"Shot? You mean again?" Dana clutched Cody's jacket in her fists, willing herself to be calm, not to care, but her heart didn't listen. It beat so hard and fast it was painful to breathe.

Dev cocked his head and looked down at her. "So he told you about the booby trap? That surprises me."

"Booby trap? What booby trap?" Dana scooted past Dev and looked in the door of the apartment. What she saw there stole the last dregs of her sanity. "Oh, my God…"

Right inside the front door was a chair with a revolver tied to its ladder-back. The cord coiled around the hammer and down to the trigger. More cord hung limply between the open door and the gun. Even more tangled piles of cord coiled around the chair legs. Dana looked down at the floor. Several black spots marred the wood finish. *Cody's blood.*

Dev put his arm loosely around her shoulders. "Gruesome, eh?" he remarked, indicating the booby trap with his expressive hands. "He must have pushed the door open and felt the resistance, then thrown himself sideways."

Dana looked at the intricate setup, and knew the terror Cody must have known when he opened the door and realized he'd stepped into a booby trap.

"Too slow," she whispered in shock, looking back at the drops of blood on the floor. She could see it in her mind's eye as if it were happening right in front of her in slow motion—the bullet traveling through the air, tearing into his arm, then bursting out through the skin on the other side. She lifted a trembling hand to her mouth.

"You got that right," Dev said, shaking his head. "The tough guy should have beat that bullet, I guarantee. Must have had something on his mind."

"Something on his mind," she repeated, and a hollow laugh escaped her lips.

Dev looked at her strangely.

Her earring. "He was thinking about me." That was why his reflexes had been too slow to dodge the bullet. Her stomach heaved alarmingly and she grabbed at Dev as she swayed.

"Dana? Here, why don't you sit yourself down." Dev gently tried to push her down to the floor.

"No," she said, licking dry lips. "I don't want to sit down. I knew Cody was shot. He came to my apartment last night. But he didn't tell me about the booby trap."

"So he's on his way over here?"

Dana shook her head, staring at the gun barrel. "I don't know. He didn't say where he was going." The black hole from which the bullet had emerged looked bottomless. She turned around slowly.

"Dana? You okay?"

"Cody said he heard the bullet hit the wall behind him," she muttered. Sure enough, imbedded in the wall was a bloodstained bullet. Dana's legs almost gave way again. She leaned on Dev.

"Olsen, get over here," Dev yelled. He nodded toward the wall. "There's your bullet," he said coldly.

The other officer turned pink, then took his knife and dug into the wall.

Dev turned his attention back to Dana. "You and Cody spent the night together?" His black eyes held amusement and affection.

She shook her head. "It's not what you think. He left this morning, furious."

Dev shook his head in wonder. "When are you two going to quit fighting and get back to loving? You're perfect for each other, you know."

"Don't, Dev, please." Dana swallowed, fear and heartache tasting like acid in her mouth. "Do you…?"

Dev raised his brows.

She tried again. "Do you think Fontenot did this?"

Dev's black gaze held hers for a long heartbeat. "Cody thinks so." He shrugged. "So that's good enough for me."

Dana laid a hand on the big detective's forearm. "Help him, Dev. Help him catch that bastard. Don't let Fontenot kill him."

"Hey, now…" Dev pulled her into the circle of his arm and gave her a quick hug. "Me, I care about the guy, too."

She didn't even protest the implication behind the word "too." She just squeezed her eyes shut and accepted his comfort. "It's just that…he thinks he's invulnerable, you know? I'm so scared that one day…"

"Don't worry, sugar. I swear I'll—" He paused and looked past her down the hall.

"There's the man now. Where y'at, Cody?" he called out in a broad Cajun accent.

Dana looked up to see Cody striding toward her.

"What the hell are you doing here?" he barked.

She flushed and pulled away from Dev's reassuring strength, and thrust the jacket toward Cody, feeling a bewildering mixture of fury and relief to see him whole, or nearly so, after her imagination had run wild.

"Here," she said shortly. "All I wanted to do was

give you your jacket back. I didn't know I'd be treated to the spectacle of how Cody Maxwell, defender of the universe, got himself all shot up!'' She licked her lips and swallowed hard.

''I see now why you didn't want to tell me. My God, Cody, if you'd been a split second slower, the bullet would have caught you right in the chest....'' She'd started out accusing him, but saying it somehow made it more real, and the edge of her vision turned black. Her fingers tingled, grew numb. The sounds around her turned to a soft buzz, fading in and out as the room began to whirl.

''Come on *chère,* sit down,'' a voice was coaxing her, buzzing in her ear like a pesky bee. She waved at it, trying to frighten it away.

''Sit down, Dana. Lean your head down. That's good.'' The voice continued, soothing, calming, as familiar, beloved hands cradled her forehead. ''Now take a deep breath. Good. Okay. Just keep breathing deeply. This is exactly why I didn't tell you. I knew you'd just get all upset.''

Dana's head slowly cleared and the debilitating nausea and dizziness faded. She swallowed, then took another deep breath. That breath was easier, then the next one was easier still.

Finally she felt as if she could raise her head without throwing up. She pushed his hands away and wiped sweat-dampened hair off her forehead and cheeks.

Cody stared down at her, his face closed and grim.

''This is all your fault, you know,'' she said.

He nodded and half smiled, a pale phantom of his usual flippant grin. ''I know. So did you call your sister? Are you going to stay with her like I suggested?''

She glared at him, still trying to regain her dignity after her ridiculous display of weakness. ''I told you, I have plans,'' she croaked. ''You could have told me what happened here. You were right about Fontenot, weren't you? This is his work.''

''I shouldn't have gotten myself shot. Now, where are you going? To your sister's, I hope.'' He put his arm around her shoulders and prepared to help her up.

Dana stiffened and scrunched her shoulders, and Cody backed off. He leaned against the wall.

''My man, you look like a zombie,'' Dev said, peering at Cody closely. ''How bad are you shot?''

Cody shrugged and winced. ''I told you, Dev, it's just a flesh wound. No problem.''

''Oh, yeah? Then why does your face look like a green tomato?''

Dana looked up. Cody did look sick, as sick as she had felt just a few minutes ago. She opened her mouth to say so, when a booming voice cut off her thoughts.

''Maxwell! What the hell are you doing?''

Cody turned and stood up straight, although Dana could see the effort it cost him.

''Captain, sir. I'm just—I was just about to take my wife home.''

''Ex-wife,'' Dana muttered, but nobody paid any attention to her.

''You want to tell me why you left the scene of a crime, for starters?''

''My wife was in danger, sir.''

''*Ex*-wife,'' she mumbled again, and heard a suspiciously amused snort coming from behind her, where Dev stood.

Captain Hamilton spared her a glance, then turned back to Cody. Dana saw the indulgent affection on the captain's florid face before he frowned again. "I'd suggest you and your *wife* get down to the station before I decide to arrest you for interfering with an investigation."

Dana opened her mouth to protest, but Captain Hamilton glared at her.

"Yes, sir," Cody said, and moved to stand next to her.

Dana stood, swallowing against a last dreg of nausea, and lifted her chin. "I'm ready," she said as the captain turned on his heel and headed back down the stairs with not so much as a glance at the crime scene.

"Come on," Cody said. "We'll go in my car."

"No!" Dana stopped.

"Dana, please. You're in no condition to drive."

"Well neither are you. I'll drive my own car. I don't want to be stranded on the other side of Canal Street with only you to depend on to get me back to my car."

"Fine." Cody headed down the stairs.

Captain Hamilton stepped around her. "Ms. Maxwell, if you insist on driving your own car, you stick close to your husband." He followed Cody down the stairs.

Dana raised a hand. "Ex…" she started, then gave up and let her arm drop. "Yes, sir," she said dryly to the closed stairwell door.

Chapter Five

Fontenot sat in the bar on St. Peter, drinking coffee and holding a newspaper. He turned the page and folded the paper, then took another sip of the strong, sweet coffee.

The tools he'd needed to install his latest creation weighed down his jacket pocket, and the heft was comforting. His lips twitched as a movement at the entryway to Maxwell's apartment caught his attention. He raised his eyes without moving his head.

The excitement began to build within him. He'd been right again. Maxwell and his wife both showed up at the crime scene this morning. His instincts were as razor sharp as ever. Now, in just a few moments, the next step in his plan would be executed. He savored the heady anticipation that flowed through his veins like a drug.

He didn't move a muscle, except to lift the cup to his mouth, as he watched the players in the drama he'd set into motion take their places.

Mrs. Maxwell, looking pale but composed, walked toward her car. Maxwell headed for his car, his attention on his wife. The police captain and the big Cajun detective came out together, and stood talking on the banquette.

Fontenot's blood throbbed in his veins with the familiar, sensual heat that only the power gave him—the power he held over life and death. He tensed his thigh muscles, and controlled his shuddering breath as Mrs. Maxwell opened her car door. In another few seconds they would all understand that he held their lives in his hands.

DANA CLIMBED INTO HER CAR, trying to ignore Cody, who stood by his own car watching her. She realized she was still carrying his jacket. She tossed it into the back seat, shot a glare in Cody's direction and sighed. She would get no peace until she'd satisfied Captain Hamilton and Cody. With an exasperated glance toward her car's clock, she slipped the key into the ignition and turned it.

Suddenly, her world exploded into light—blinding light, flashing all around her. Instinctively she cringed, waiting for the inevitable explosion.

A strong hand dragged her from the car and threw her onto the ground. Then a huge weight fell on her and they rolled over and over. Stones and rough pavement bruised her back, and she would have bumped her head, except that a warm palm cradled it.

Cody groaned with pain, then scrambled up and jerked her up. "Come on!" he shouted.

Dana ran with him. She stumbled, caught herself, stumbled again, until finally Cody pulled her abruptly up against his chest. His heart pounded fiercely, just like hers.

"Are you all right?" he whispered raggedly in her ear, his voice hoarse and unsteady. His whole body shuddered, and he crushed her so tight she couldn't breathe.

"I think so," she gasped. "Wh-what was that?"

Cody took a deep breath, his chest swelling against her breasts. "I thought it was a bomb. God, Dana! I thought you were dead." His arm tightened convulsively around her.

Dana stared at him, stunned, as his words sank in. "A bomb?"

Cody took another long breath as Dev grabbed both of them.

"You guys okay?" Dev's voice was as breathless and hoarse as Cody's.

"Damn, man," the big Cajun continued. "I thought—"

"What was it, Dev?" Cody asked, turning Dana loose.

She swayed and caught herself.

Dev and Cody headed toward the car.

"Cody, don't—" But as usual, no one was listening to her. She followed at a distance as the two men cautiously approached her car. Cody pushed his fingers through his hair and wiped his face. Dev's face was pale under his black hair and beard.

Uniformed policemen swarmed over the car, and Dana heard one of them shout as he knelt beside the car. "Here's the trigger."

Cody glanced back at her, then followed Dev. She stepped closer, in time to hear Dev's words.

"It was nothing but a lot of light, Code. Tiny flashbulbs going off around the dashboard." Dev let out a string of curses that would have embarrassed Dana, if she hadn't been so dazed and shaken by the explosion of light.

Cody doubled his fist and hit the fender. "That son of a bitch!" he cursed between his teeth.

"Cody?" Dana squeaked.

He turned around and held out his arms. She stepped into his embrace and squeezed her eyes shut. The echo of the flashing lights still burned behind her closed lids. She let her head rest in the hollow between his neck and shoulder just for a moment. She felt safe there.

"What was it?" she asked, her words muffled by the cloth of his shirt.

He put one hand on the back of her head, gently holding her. For a fleeting instant she wished she could stay there forever, safe in Cody's arms.

"That bastard Fontenot. He rigged your car with flashbulbs."

"Flashbulbs? Are you serious?" Dana pulled away as reality intruded into her brief fantasy of safety. "I wasn't away from the car but a few minutes."

"That's right, Code. She couldn't have gotten there more than five minutes before you." Dev's deep voice came from behind her. "There's no way he could have done it. Look around. There are uniforms everywhere."

Cody clenched his fists and anger suffused his features. "Well *he* did it. Don't you get it? He rigged it right out here in the open, in front of everybody. It's another message. Dana could have been blown apart. The trigger for those flashbulbs could have just as easily been a bomb." His arms tightened reflexively around her.

"But they weren't," she protested weakly, shivering as she grasped the full implication of what Fontenot had done, and saw the dark intensity of Cody's gaze.

"A bomb..." she whispered, shaking her head. "In my car. But why? Cody, why? I never did anything to the man."

Cody grabbed her shoulders and shook her slightly. "Dana, get it through your head. It's because of me. It's because he thinks you mean something to me. His only motive is to get at me, and he thinks he can do that through you." He set her aside as if she were nothing more than a hat rack.

That's exactly what she felt like. An inanimate object, something that could be used by Fontenot in revenge against Cody. But his plan would work only if she meant something to Cody. Cody's harsh words echoed in her ears.

It's because he thinks you mean something to me.

But of course she didn't. Nothing meant anything to Cody except his job. She knew that. She'd known it for a long time, and she'd do well not to forget it.

Dev and Cody walked back toward the car, talking to the uniformed officers and inspecting the fake bomb made of flashbulbs that had been pulled out from under the car.

Her car looked perfectly innocuous now. She shuddered. Maybe it would be a good idea to visit her sister in Pensacola. She'd be safe there.

Cody's head was bent over the bundle of wires and bulbs, and he was pulling on latex gloves. She could tell by his stiff movements that his shoulder was hurting.

She could leave town, but what would Cody do? Where would he be safe? Dana lifted her chin. It didn't matter, she reminded herself. It didn't matter to her what he did. He was no longer her responsibility.

"Maxwell!" a deep, resonant voice boomed. "Get your butt over here!"

Dana looked around to see the captain in an unmarked police car.

"You, too, Mrs. Maxwell. Get in the car."

There was no brooking the authority in his voice, so Dana got into the police captain's car and scooted across the back seat as Cody got in beside her.

An hour and a half later, Dana was frustrated, and hot, and thirsty. She regretted refusing the muddy precinct house coffee, she was tired of sitting on the hard wooden chair, and if the young officer taking her statement didn't start using more than two fingers to type, she thought she might scream.

Finally, he finished painstakingly typing her last answer on the ancient electric typewriter, with only two erasures, and yanked the sheet of paper.

"Now, Mrs. Maxwell, if you'll just sign here."

Dana resisted her lawyer's urge to read back over the statement. She'd gone over the events of last night and this morning at least a dozen times, and she did not want to take the chance of having to go over them a thirteenth time. Grabbing the pen, she dashed off her signature and dated the document. "May I leave now?"

The officer swallowed, and cut his eyes around to the captain's office. Just as he did, Cody walked in with his arm in a sling.

He looked pale, and his eyes looked tired.

"Cody…"

He came over to where she was sitting, flashing a

faded version of his angelic grin. "Hey, *chère*. Have they finished grilling you? No rubber hoses, I hope."

Dana opened her mouth, but she didn't even get a chance to squeak.

"Maxwell! Get in here. Bring your wife."

"Ex—" *Oh, what was the use?* She sighed and stood.

Cody placed his hand on the small of her back and guided her into the captain's office, where Dev leaned on the windowsill.

"Did you get patched up, Maxwell?"

"Yes, sir."

"All right then." Captain Hamilton sat up in his chair. "Sit down, Mrs. Maxwell. Now, given what's happened, last night and today, I think the best idea is for you and your wife to vacate the area until we've apprehended Gerard Fontenot."

Cody tensed. "Captain—"

"Shut up, Maxwell. Now, we need to put you two in a safe house."

"I'm staying here."

Dev spoke. "Get real, Code. You're injured."

"It's just a flesh wound. I know Fontenot. I need to be in on this. Get Dana out of town. But let me stay."

"Out of the question," the captain growled.

"But—"

"Maxwell, I'm warning you. Now, Gautier. Where can we put them?"

Dev opened his mouth, but Dana took a deep breath and broke in. "Captain, excuse me, but don't I have a say in what's going on here?"

The captain glowered at her.

She continued before he could say no. "I could go to Pensacola, to my sister's."

All three men glared at her.

"What?"

Cody put his hand on her shoulder. Its warmth seeped into her and she had to fight to keep from leaning toward him, toward the safety his warm body promised. *He's not safe. He's dangerous.*

"Dana, it's too risky. Fontenot probably knows all about your sister."

"But you said—"

"I was wrong." His face was grim as he looked down at her. "I don't want to underestimate him."

Again. The unspoken word hung in the air.

"Fontenot's lived in New Orleans all his life. We can't take a chance that he'll know our safe houses," Dev commented. "The man seems to be super-human."

Dana put her hand over Cody's. "What about the lake house?" she asked.

Cody glanced at her, then at Dev. "It could work. It's in her grandfather's best friend's name. He's in a nursing home. It's not connected with us, and it's on the north shore of the Pontchartrain."

"You could be followed," Captain Hamilton said, just as his phone rang.

He picked it up and listened. "Is that confirmed?"

Dana waited tensely. She could feel a similar tension in Cody and Dev. She licked her lips.

Hamilton put the phone receiver down and looked at Cody. "We just got word that Fontenot rented a car."

Cody frowned. "How'd we find that out?"

"I've had an all-points out on all flights, trains and

rental car agencies. Now, listen. He asked for a map of Pensacola.''

''Angie,'' Dana breathed, in alarm. ''Oh, God, Cody. He's going to Angie's.''

Cody's fingers squeezed her shoulder reassuringly. ''Don't worry, *chère,* we'll alert the Pensacola police.''

''All right, Maxwell. You two get a move on. Take one of the unmarked cars. And leave complete info on this lake house of yours. Now, get going.'' He picked up the phone. ''Get me the chief of police in Pensacola. Now!''

Two hours later Cody and Dana were at the lake house. Dana pulled the last bag of groceries out of the trunk of the unmarked police car as Cody unlocked the cabin door. She pushed past him into the tiny kitchen. ''I still can't help worrying about Angie,'' she muttered as she unpacked milk and coffee and oranges.

''Don't. The captain alerted Pensacola police, and Dev's driving over there himself. They'll take care of her.''

''Oh, yeah? Like they took care of you? I don't see why Captain Hamilton had to send you up here.''

''Hey, I'm not thrilled to be here. I need to be back in New Orleans, helping with the investigation. They don't understand Fontenot like I do. Damn!'' Cody tossed the other grocery bags onto the counter, then headed back out the door.

''Where are you going?'' she asked.

''I thought I'd take a look around.''

''The doctor said you needed to rest and drink lots of liquids to make up for the blood you lost.''

''Dana,'' he said with deliberate patience. ''There

is a madman out there who wants to kill me, and he won't mind killing you to get to me. So I think I'll just take a look around to be sure nobody followed us.''

Dana laughed. ''Are you kidding? Followed us? The way you were driving? Besides, isn't that why we're here? Because Fontenot couldn't possibly know about this place?''

''Indulge me, counselor. Pretend I'm checking for mildew or dry rot or something.''

''Fine,'' she said, waving a bunch of carrots at him. ''Go. I don't care if your shoulder starts bleeding again if you don't. Go play detective. I'm going to start supper. I haven't eaten anything all day.'' As Cody disappeared through the door, she turned her attention back to the vegetables she was pulling out of the grocery sack.

She wasn't happy at all with Captain Hamilton's suggestion that she and Cody stay at the lake for three or four days while the police tracked down Fontenot. Suggestion—ha! Order was more like it. She rinsed two tomatoes and began peeling them.

How was she going to stay here with Cody for three days? Three whole days of his know-it-all attitude, and his laughing blue eyes and his angelic smile. Dana stopped her thoughts right there. Captain Hamilton could have just as easily sent another officer up here with her, and sent Cody somewhere else. Anywhere else.

But no. The captain had ordered them up here together. Dana reluctantly admitted to herself that he was right on two counts. Cody needed to be away from New Orleans and Dana felt safer with Cody than she would have with anyone else. She smiled reluctantly. It was fairly obvious the captain had an ulterior motive, too. He wanted to get Cody out of his hair while they tracked down Fontenot. Cody wouldn't be much help with a wounded shoulder, but the captain obviously knew her husband. *Ex-husband,* she corrected herself. Cody would want to be right in the middle of the investigation.

"So I'm a glorified, unpaid baby-sitter, right?" She stuck a piece of tomato in her mouth.

Three days with Cody. It was a good thing she wasn't vulnerable to his charm anymore. She was over him. She dried her hands and walked through the kitchen into the single bedroom.

Everything looked to be in pretty good shape. She folded the bedspread back and smoothed the sheets, taking a deep breath. The air was fresh and cool, no mildew.

She plumped the pillows, then smoothed her palms across the soft, worn cotton. The last time they'd been up here together was the weekend they'd made their baby.

Pain slashed through her breast like a sabre. Her breath caught. She sank to the edge of the bed and pulled a pillow into her arms, hugging it like she would have hugged their baby, if it had ever been born. The pain and grief flared briefly, reminding her that it had been there, dull and constant, ever since the night of her miscarriage.

Deep inside, in her secret heart, she knew it was unfair to blame Cody. People lost babies all the time, didn't they?

That's really all it was, an unfortunate miscarriage, even if it had coincided with the night Fontenot shot Cody.

There are dozens of reasons for miscarriages, Mrs. Maxwell, the doctor had said kindly, as he'd patted her hand. *Women often miscarry in the first month or so and never even know they were pregnant.* He'd carefully explained that she would have probably miscarried, anyway, and that early miscarriages generally indicated that the fetus was defective.

Fetus. She'd wanted to scream then, and she wanted to scream now. It wasn't a fetus, it was her baby. Their baby.

She'd only missed one period, so she'd hardly been pregnant at all. Still, the pain had stayed, the pain of loss, of loneliness, of shattered dreams. And facing the death of her baby and the near death of her husband had been too much to take all at once.

She'd forgotten all the memories that were stored inside these walls.

"*Chère,* you okay?"

Cody's voice penetrated the cloud of memories surrounding her. She stood abruptly, tossing the pillow onto the bed and clearing her throat. "Sure. I'm fine." She composed her face, then turned to look at him.

He stood framed in the doorway, his mouth set and his eyes dark, as if he were hurting.

"Are you ready to eat?"

He shook his head. "Not right now. You sure you're okay?"

"I really think you should eat something."

He stepped toward her, glancing toward the bed then back at her face. "Dana, what were you doing?"

"Just…just checking the sheets for mildew. Everything's fine."

"No, everything's not fine." He touched her shoulder.

Dana ducked out of his reach, panic swelling her chest. "Yes. Yes, it is."

"You were remembering the last time we were up here, weren't you?"

She shook her head jerkily. "No. No, I—"

He stepped closer, and tucked a stray tendril of her hair behind her ear. "It's okay. I remember, too. I'm sorry, *chère*. If it would help to talk, you know I'm here for you."

"Really?" she asked, her voice sharp. "That's funny. It seems to me you're right where you've always been, on the edge of danger. Not here with me at all."

"Don't do this, Dana. Not to me. Not to yourself."

"Do what?" She pulled away again and headed for the door. "I was just checking the sheets. Now, I'm going to fix supper. You look tired."

Cody's blue eyes flashed, then went dull. "I'm okay," he said in a low voice. "Everything looks fine around the cabin. I'm going to walk down to the lake."

"Damn it, Cody. You never take care of yourself. You look like you haven't slept in a week, you're pale and shaky, and you've worn the same clothes for two days. Why don't you take a shower and go to bed? You need some rest."

He just stood there, his arms crossed, a wry smile curving his lips. "You know, *chère,* you don't have to tell me what I need. Especially since you can't even admit your own needs. I can take care of myself. I'm all grown up now."

An unreasonable fury trembled inside her, desperate to be released. She let it all out—all the fear and anger and worry she'd bottled up ever since he'd walked into her apartment bleeding and hurt. "All grown up? Cody Maxwell? I don't think so. You're still playing cops and robbers. You still think your life is some television drama where the good guys always win." She wrapped her arms around herself and scrunched her shoulders.

"I'm tired of you accusing me of treating my job like some kind of game, Dana. I'm a cop. I *am* a good guy. This is not a game, it's life and death, and I'd like to think I'm helping the good guys win."

"You're not winning! You're not invincible. Look at you. You keep getting shot, keep getting closer to that last inevitable bullet that's going to kill you." She could feel the tears clogging the back of her throat, tears of anger, of fear, of unbearable pain. She swallowed them.

She would not cry. She would not show him how much it hurt her to see him struggling against corruption, like a lonely champion. It broke her heart to know he really believed he was invincible, that he could save the world without getting himself killed.

"Why couldn't you just live a normal, quiet life, Cody? Why wasn't that enough for you?"

Cody's face had gone blank as she'd yelled. He stood up straight, his eyes hooded and a small frown creasing his forehead. "I'm going for that walk. But please, don't let that stop you. I wouldn't want to spoil your fun. It's been four years since you've had a chance to yell at me, so pretend I'm still here. Seems like old times, doesn't it?"

His voice was so bitter, so hard.

"Are you saying I'm wrong?" she shouted at him. "I'm just stating the facts. You think you've got some invisible shield around you. Just like Dev said, you think bullets bounce off you.''

She was becoming hysterical, and her throat was clogging up. She swallowed hard. ''Well, look at the scar on your head, Cody. Look at your arm. That bullet didn't bounce off. What happened to your invisible shield this time?''

''Maybe you've put too many cracks in it with your razor-sharp tongue.'' He turned on his heel and stalked out of the house.

Dana went into the bathroom and ran cold water over her wrists, then splashed her face. She stood there, her dripping hands covering her face, until the back of her throat stopped hurting with the need to cry.

He wasn't being fair. If he'd stop his one-man crusade to save the world for a minute, he'd see what he was doing to himself and to her.

What had happened to them? Once he'd been her knight in shining armor, strong enough to slay all the dragons. Once he'd thought she was beautiful—gorgeous, he'd said. Once they'd thought love was enough.

How sad to find out that it wasn't.

She went back into the kitchen and started chopping celery.

CODY WALKED DOWN to the lake and tossed pebbles into the water for a while, until the throbbing in his arm spread up to his shoulder and across his back.

As he idly skipped stones, he casually let his gaze roam over the little swampy inlet. It was isolated, quiet. Nothing unusual. Nothing suspicious. From the deck of the lake house, he'd seen the winding dirt road that led up here. The waters of Lake Pontchartrain stretched off to the horizon, but the trees hid most of the lake house from view, making it a perfect hideout.

After a while, he turned and walked back up the bank to the deck that spanned the front of the little cabin. He sat down on the top step and leaned back against the rail, trying to find a comfortable position for his shoulder. He hated to admit it, but he did feel a little better now that the wounds were stitched up.

He heard Dana in the kitchen, scurrying around like a mouse making its nest. A smile played involuntarily around his mouth.

She was something, all right. So competent, so organized. All that order made him crazy. He shook his head.

But somehow, it was also comforting, like knowing there was a haven he could go to if the world got too chaotic for him. He missed that.

And that wasn't all he missed. He missed the rosy scent of her hair, the soft swell of her breasts, the cloudy verdure of her eyes when he made love to her. That magical moment when he made it past what he called her point of no return. His body tightened in response to his thoughts. When he got past her veneer of control, she was the sexiest, most gorgeous thing he'd ever touched. He remembered the first time they'd ever made love, right after they met. He'd teased her about her day planner, and written in it *make love with Cody*. Her slow awakening under his gentle hands had been one of the reasons he'd fallen in love with her. Nothing had ever turned him on more than making love with his wife.

He threw the pebble he'd been toying with, and tried to wipe away the image of her beneath him, mouth parted in anticipation, body quivering in response to him.

Why couldn't she just accept him for what he was? Even as his brain formed the question, he knew the answer.

They were too different. She had never understood what being a cop meant to him. She'd never taken the responsibility seriously. His father had been a cop, and his grandfather. It was in his blood, it was his heritage. His father had never turned his back on his duty. Cody's mother had always understood that. She'd waited for her husband, until the day she died, a year before his dad.

Dana had wanted safety and security more than she wanted him. She'd presented him with an impossible choice—his honor or her. He couldn't give her the kind of safe, bland existence she wanted and remain true to himself. As long as she was with him, she'd never have what she wanted.

How well he knew that.

It had broken his heart earlier, when he saw the sadness in her face as she sat on the bed, clutching the pillow. He knew exactly what she was thinking, why she was bowed with grief. It didn't take a rocket scientist to figure out that she'd gotten pregnant that last weekend they were here.

They'd come here to give themselves a chance to patch things up. But they'd argued and bickered the whole weekend, except when they'd made love.

There in the living room, in front of a roaring fire, they'd made a baby. Then less than two months later, while he'd been in surgery having a bullet dug out of his brain, she'd miscarried.

She blamed him. And why not? He blamed himself.

Cody leaned his head back against the deck rail and closed his eyes, trying to drag his thoughts away from hurtful memories.

He heard a cry and a curse from the kitchen.

Chapter Six

Rushing inside, Cody found Dana standing at the kitchen counter, a paring knife in one hand and an onion in the other. The hand holding the onion was bleeding.

She looked up at him, tears shining in her eyes.

"Here, *chère,* let me see." He took the onion and the knife away from her, then held her finger under cold water. "It's just a nick. It'll be fine. I'll just put a Band-Aid on it."

She gasped audibly. Cody looked up, afraid he'd hurt her, but she was staring at him, her face crumpling like a child's, tears streaming down her cheeks.

He pulled her into his arms. "It's okay. You're okay. Don't cry."

She strained against his hold. "I'm—not crying," she said in a small, choked voice. "It's the onions."

"Dana," he whispered softly. "It's okay to cry, you know. You've been through a lot in the last two days. Go ahead."

"I'm—not—crying."

He put his hand on the back of her neck and massaged the stiff muscles, his compassion stirred by her determination, her rigid need to remain in control.

"Okay, okay. You're not crying," he soothed. "Not crying a bit. Just relax until the onions quit burning your eyes, okay?" He held her, rocking gently from side to side, massaging her neck, until he felt her relax, felt her erratic breathing return to normal.

"That's it. You're doing good. Just breathe. Just breathe," he whispered, saying anything that came into his head, just talking to calm her down.

She didn't like to seem vulnerable. She'd never liked to be caught crying over a sentimental movie, or a hurtful remark, or a miscarriage, he thought grimly as he continued to whisper to her. "You're doing fine, *chère*. Everything's going to be all right, just as soon as those onions quit burning."

It was something else he didn't understand about her. Didn't understand, but admired just the same. "You're doing great. So strong, so good."

She sniffled quietly. Where had all this rigid strength come from? What in her life had caused her to be so afraid of losing control?

He thought about how odd it was for her to break down like this, but then, it had been a bad week for her, to say the least. And he hadn't helped any by dragging her into this mess with Fontenot. "It won't be long," he murmured, burying his nose in her hair. "They'll catch Fontenot, then I'll take you over to your sister's. You won't have to put up with me anymore. Okay, *chère?* You'll be safe and sound there."

Dana's body began to relax against him, and suddenly, Cody found himself reacting. The rosy scent of her hair was filling his nostrils, and the exquisite feel of her molded against him brought to mind some decidedly erotic memories. His fingers slowed to a caress on her nape and he shifted, his jeans suddenly uncomfortably tight.

Dana obviously noticed, because she pulled away, wiping her eyes. "I'll get that Band-Aid," she said briskly, with just a hint of tears still in her voice.

Cody smiled at her, tamping down the desire that had caught him unawares. "I'll finish chopping that onion," he offered.

She looked up at him, a tremulous smile on her lips. "Thanks."

Cody pulled his gaze away from the doorway through which she'd gone. That was the first time she'd smiled at him since this whole thing started last night. He picked up the knife and the onion and leaned against the counter, turning them in his hands. He tossed the onion into the air and caught it.

It was nice to see her smile.

DANA DRIED HER HANDS and put a Band-Aid on her nicked finger. *How stupid, cutting herself, then crying about it.*

Okay, so she wasn't crying about the cut. She shrugged. She didn't like to cry. Crying revealed too much, to others and to herself. As long as she didn't cry, she could stay in control. As long as she didn't break down, she could keep herself removed from the hurtful parts of life. It was easier that way.

The other way, like the few moments when she'd allowed Cody to comfort her, felt too good. Letting somebody else take the pain was too easy.

Do it very often and you started to depend on them being there to help. Then it hurt even more when they were gone. She knew all about that.

Just like Cody. He'd been so sweet, so considerate.

He'd known as well as she did that the problem wasn't the tiny cut. Thank goodness he hadn't teased her about it.

Her throat tightened. She loved the sweetness that lay at the heart of him, beneath his tough competence. At one time she'd allowed herself to depend on his sweetness, his strength. She'd trusted in him like she'd not trusted anyone since she was a little girl.

Cody had always treated her with a tender humor that kept her from being too serious. When they first met, she'd thought they complemented each other, kept each other balanced. She'd loved the spontaneous side of him—the dangerous side that was tempered with his sweetness. Through him she could experience excitement and danger, knowing he would keep her safe.

But Cody's dangerous side had gotten to be too much. She'd lost her confidence in him. She couldn't be sure he'd be there.

She couldn't trust him not to die.

She looked in the mirror, at her reddened eyes and her mussed hair. She looked horrible. But then, in the past twenty-four hours she'd patched up a bleeding ex-husband, been almost blown up in her own car, and whisked away to a hideout. All in all, not a typical way to start a weekend.

"Humph." The faint light of a smile tickled the corners of her mouth. "I must be nuts to think this is funny," she muttered. Gallows humor was more Cody's style. She splashed water on her face, then went back into the kitchen.

Cody had dished up the salad and toasted the bread. They ate and then washed the dishes together, polite and a little distracted, like casual acquaintances forced together by circumstance.

After drinking two glasses of wine with dinner, Dana was overwhelmingly drowsy.

"I think I'll go to bed," she said, then suddenly roused a bit as she thought about the implications. A faint wave of anticipation rippled through her, taking her by surprise. She pushed away memories of the two of them, legs tangled, breathless with love and laughter, in that bed.

They were here for one reason only, because Captain Hamilton had given Cody an order.

"I mean—where am I going to sleep?" She looked at Cody, who was smiling crookedly at her.

"You take the bedroom," he said. "I'll sleep on the couch."

"But what about your arm?" she protested quickly. "Why don't you take the bedroom and I'll sleep on the couch. It's comfortable enough."

"I doubt I'll sleep very well, anyway. I want to stay out here and keep an eye out for anything suspicious. You go ahead."

"But you can't stay awake all night. You need your rest."

"I'll be fine, Dana. You're exhausted. Go on."

Dana looked at his pale face, his pinched mouth, and started to protest again.

"I mean it, Dana. You take the bedroom."

She knew that tone. He'd made up his mind and if she insisted she'd only make him angry. "Okay, sir," she said with a mock salute. "Understood."

She was rewarded with his angelic grin. Giving him back a wan smile, she escaped into the bedroom and pushed the door to without latching it.

As she tried to go to sleep, Cody's beautiful smile haunted her. How sweet he'd been when she cut herself. How strong and warm his arms had felt around her. How familiar his growing desire had felt against her.

A warm, tingly yearning began inside her. He'd always been able to slip behind her defenses when he made love to her, many times right here in this bed. A quiet moan escaped her lips as the yearning sharpened and deepened.

Stop it. She turned over and doubled the pillow under her head. She had to stop thinking about him if she was going to get any sleep.

It was probably natural to have some leftover erotic thoughts of her husband, she reassured herself. After all, they'd been married for two years.

And now, here they were, forced together by something beyond their control. Naturally some pleasant memories were bound to surface along with the unpleasant ones. They didn't mean anything, though. She couldn't afford to let them mean anything. They were divorced. That part of her life was over.

The good times weren't good enough to make up for the bad. Dana repeated that sentence like a mantra as she scrunched her shoulders and drew her legs up, concentrating on going to sleep.

CODY SAT UP FAR INTO the night, drinking wine. His arm throbbed a little less as he got closer to the end of the bottle. He considered opening a second bottle, but decided against it. They were in danger. He couldn't afford to forget that for a second.

Stretched out on the couch in the dark, he could see the lake through the glass doors. He liked watching

Lake Pontchartrain at night. With the moonlight glinting off its surface it looked like an eerily calm ocean, with barely a ripple disturbing the glassy smoothness of the water.

It was deceiving. Smooth and stable on the surface, but teeming with life and danger below, like the alligators that lurked just under the surface, their rough hides making them look like floating logs.

He dozed off to sleep listening to the crickets and frogs and the occasional ominous grunt of a gator.

The car exploded into flames. Cody screamed as the hot fire engulfed Dana. He could see her, a black silhouette surrounded by yellow-and-red flames, writhing in the inferno. No! Oh, God, Dana!

He jerked awake. Sitting up, he pushed his hands through his hair as he struggled to catch his breath.

It was just a dream. A nightmare. They'd been flashbulbs, not a bomb.

His heart finally quit pounding like a jackhammer against his chest wall. Fontenot was diabolical, the way he rigged his booby traps. The man was a genius, a sociopath whose intelligence was only surpassed by his cruelty.

Cody had seen the cat the fiend had strung up over his estranged wife's bed, perfectly positioned so that the blood dripped down onto the woman's pillow. He'd done it because she wouldn't go back to him. Then he'd filled her refrigerator with snakes. They hadn't been able to get a conviction for murder, even though the wife had died. Heart attack, the coroner said.

It was ironic. If Cody hadn't been so determined to prove that Fontenot had murdered his wife, Fontenot wouldn't have shot Cody. And if Fontenot hadn't shot

Cody, he and Dana might still be married, might even have a child. They might be safe.

Cody's mouth was dry. He got a glass of water and walked out onto the deck. The moon was setting, and a faint glow began in the east. He drained the glass and sat down on the top step.

Fontenot had rigged flashbulbs to the ignition switch of Dana's car, in less than ten minutes with a swarm of police around.

Suddenly Cody's hands shook. He leaned his elbows on his knees and pushed his fingers through his hair.

Pictures of Dana flashed through his mind, one after another, as if lit by the firing flashbulbs.

Dana drinking coffee, her hair tangled and her eyes hazy with sleep.

Dana emerging from the water, glistening drops shining on the tops of her creamy white breasts.

Dana, staring up at him with tears in her eyes as he told her everything was all right, knowing all the while he was lying, and knowing she knew it.

She might have died.

He put his palms against his closed eyelids. His eyes burned like fire, like hot tears. He rubbed his eyes, then leaned his head back against the railing and stared up at the moon. He tried to swallow the lump of fear that was stuck in his throat. Not fear for himself. Fear for Dana. She had innocently turned that key. It was as simple as that.

Click.

Boom.

The setting moon swam dizzily in his vision, and Cody felt something wet run down his cheek, tickling as it ran.

A thought occurred to him. This was what Dana had gone through, day after day, night after endless night while she waited for him to come home. This was how she'd felt, sitting alone, waiting to find out if the bullet Fontenot had put into his brain would kill him. For the first time, Cody understood, in a way he never had before, why she'd left him.

He sat there, helpless, while the vision of the flashing lights played over and over in his head. Every time it played, he felt again the agonizing terror, the split second of unbearable horror, while he waited for the explosion that he was powerless to stop.

After a while, he closed his eyes and tears dripped down his cheeks. He sniffed and blinked, but they just kept coming.

Another realization came to him. This was why she didn't like to cry. Crying made you feel so damned helpless, so vulnerable, so out of control. So Cody, a man who'd never cried in his life, wept silently, helplessly, without really knowing how.

A long time later, he went inside. He quietly pushed open the bedroom door. In the gray half light of dawn he could see Dana, all curled in on herself, sleeping as if her life depended on it. It was his fault she was so tense. His fault that she couldn't relax, even in sleep.

He watched her for a while, just to reassure himself that she was truly all right. Then, quietly and slowly, he lay down on the bed beside her.

She stirred and turned over, pushing back against him the way they used to sleep long ago, when they were in love. Desire stirred in him, familiar as a lingering taste of wine or something sweet.

But what awed him and frightened the wits out of

him was the way her body relaxed, molding against his, in innocent, unconscious trust. She'd been tense and rigid, but in sleep, instinctively, she trusted him, and her body relaxed.

His throat ached with emotion, but he swallowed hard and draped his arm over her waist. He was beginning to understand more and more about his wife.

And he was beginning to realize how much he'd missed her, because, for the first time in four years, for the first time since she'd last lain beside him, Cody felt like he could sleep peacefully.

He closed his eyes, comforted by her presence, and wondered how long it would take Fontenot to find them.

A BIRD SCREECHED right outside the window, pulling Dana into the day. She stretched and turned over, burrowing her nose into Cody's back and slipping her arm around his waist from behind. She snuggled up against the curve of his spine and dozed, secure in the knowledge that he was home, safe.

The bird screeched again, and the low, faraway grunt of an alligator floated in the window on the breeze. A dawning consciousness of the room around her woke her a little more. They were at the lake house. She yawned and snuggled in closer to Cody's warm back. Something wasn't quite right.

Then she woke up enough to remember that they were divorced and he shouldn't be in bed with her.

She jerked away and sat up. "Cody! What are you doing here?"

Cody jumped, then cursed. "Ouch!"

He grimaced and sat up gingerly, cradling his left arm. Dana looked at the bandage on his arm, then at his pale, drawn face. She'd forgotten where they were, forgotten about his wound. For a minute there, snuggled against his warm, hard body the way she'd always loved to sleep, she'd forgotten a lot of things, like the last four years.

"Sorry," she grumbled ungraciously, "but what are you doing in my bed?"

His face turned red and he tossed back the covers and got up. "I came in to check on you," he said shortly.

Dana hardly heard what he said. She already knew he had no shirt on, because she'd woken up with her cheek resting on his bare back, and her breasts pressed against his sleep-warmed skin. But all that covered him were a pair of boxer shorts. Her eyes scanned the long, lean body she'd once known as well as her own, the delicious curve of his back, the well-shaped buttocks that looked so great in jeans, his long legs.

"Check on me? For what?" She didn't like the idea that he thought she needed checking on. Slowly, all the events of the day before came back to her. Her heart sped up. "Did something happen? Did you hear something?"

He turned around at the door and looked at her with those incredible blue eyes that could still stop her heart. "No, Dana. It was late. I looked in on you, and lay down for a minute and fell asleep. Pardon me."

He glared at her for a second, then turned on his heel and went out into the living room, leaving Dana staring at the empty doorway. His body was still lean and hard, loose-limbed and graceful. She shook her head. She was going to have to stop letting her brain think about Cody that way—like a woman thinks about a man. They were divorced. There was nothing between them anymore. It was just the enforced close-ness here where some of their best times had taken place that was confusing her.

She jumped out of bed and put on shorts and a T-shirt and slipped her feet into backless sandals. Of course, it would help if he wouldn't parade around naked and climb in her bed while she was asleep.

That thought triggered others, like the warm, sleepy smell of his skin, like the delicious hardness of his body against her when she'd drowsily snuggled up against him.

This wasn't going to work, she decided as she ran a brush through her hair and splashed water on her face. She couldn't stay here. There were too many memories.

Dev had mentioned a safe house. She'd ask Cody about that today, a neutral place, where they could stay without being constantly bombarded by the past. She took a deep breath and strode into the kitchen.

Cody had pulled on jeans, but he was still barefoot and bare-chested. He was pouring boiling water into a cup. "Coffee?" he said, filling another cup.

Dana frowned. "I guess so. I wish you'd have let me get some fresh ground." She took the cup from him and sat down at the ancient wooden table.

"We didn't have time. You know that."

"Oh, come on, Cody. Of course we had time. The way you drive? I wanted to try that new pecan praline coffee. I had a coupon for it. It's important to save money." She took a sip from her cup and grimaced. "Perked coffee is so much better."

Cody turned his back on her and stood at the kitchen door, looking out as he sipped the hot liquid. "Right.

Saving money is what's important," he said sarcastically, "and, oh yeah, you had a coupon, too."

"I don't know what you're so grouchy about," she grumbled, remembering how irritated he'd been when she'd pulled the coupons out of her planner. "It doesn't take any more time to be practical. My grocery store pays double the value on coupons. I could have saved two dollars."

Cody whirled around. "Damn it, Dana, this isn't about coupons. It isn't about saving money. It's about life and death." He slammed his cup down on the table and leaned over her, his face ominously dark, his hands on either side of her gripping the arms of her chair. "You shop with coupons to save a dollar, but when you leave town you announce it to the whole city on your answering machine."

Dana bit her lip and shrank back against the chair. Cody could be intimidating when he wanted to be. "It was two dollars," she said in a voice that was much more quavery than she'd intended it to be. "And I'm sick of hearing about my answering machine. I'm out of town a lot, and my clients deserve to know when they can reach me."

"Your *clients* don't deserve to know all the details of your life. You have to take precautions. Especially now."

He leaned in until his face was no more than an inch from hers. She could see the sparks of anger in his blue eyes, could feel the fury emanating from him like fever, and she shrank back even more.

"You are a piece of work. Haven't you figured it out yet? You gave Fontenot all the information he needed. He knew you were out of town. He got into your apartment and took your earring out from under your bed.'' His face was so close to hers she could feel his breath on her lips.

''Think about it, Dana. Fontenot walked on your floor. He touched your things. The man who killed his own wife, the man who shot me, went through your things. He probably touched your clothes. Maybe even your pillow. And he left without you ever knowing he'd been there. You think it's important to let your clients know where to reach you? You want to take a little extra time to save two dollars? He could have killed you. I think you've got your priorities all screwed up, counselor.''

Dana shuddered at the picture Cody painted of Fontenot touching her things. The idea terrified her, and she lashed out. ''I've got *my* priorities screwed up? Why don't you talk about why this man is after us in the first place? He's after us because you couldn't let the justice system work. You couldn't sit back like a normal human being and expect a jury to convict him. No. You had to be judge, jury and executioner. Cody Maxwell had to go after the bad guy and get himself shot in the head for his trouble.''

She pushed against him and he pulled away. She stood.

''You walked into that bullet, Cody. You walked right into it, because just like always, you thought you were smarter than the whole justice system. You thought you were the only one who could do it right. And you think I've got *my* priorities screwed up?''

''The man tried to murder you. Just what do you think my damn priorities ought to be? Saving my own ass, or putting away a dangerous sociopath who's trying to kill my wife?''

''Ex-wife,'' she said quietly as Cody straightened

suddenly and grabbed his coffee, downing it in one gulp. Dana breathed a sigh of relief that he'd backed off. She picked up her cup, sloshing coffee over the side. She grabbed it with both hands and held it in front of her like a shield.

"You have no right to get in my face like that," she challenged him. "You know you scare me when you get so angry."

"I'm not angry," he said shortly, banging the cup down on the counter.

Dana jumped.

"Damn," he muttered. "Don't act so scared. You know I'd never hurt you."

Dana's heart twisted. Of course he wouldn't. Not physically. She'd never been afraid of him. "I know. It's just, around you, everything is so...intense. You're so, I don't know, passionate, about everything. Your job, your leisure time, your—" She stopped. She'd been about to say, *your lovemaking.*

She knew he knew what she'd almost said. His manner changed. Suddenly the anger was gone, and he was looking at her in that way he did, his eyes heavy-lidded and deep cobalt blue. Her face heated, and her gaze faltered.

"Go ahead, *chère*," he murmured, his voice rumbling through her like faraway thunder. "Tell me what else I'm passionate about."

"Don't," she said, stiffening. She was too raw, too vulnerable, after waking up next to him two mornings in a row. She fought for the control that was so important to her, and that Cody could so easily breach with an offhand grin or a smoky look.

He shrugged, the movement rippling the muscles of

his shoulders and drawing her attention to the bandage on his arm.

His expression went blank and he shook his head slightly. "I'm going to take a shower."

"Good," Dana retorted, irritated that her voice shook. She took a deep breath. "It's about time you cleaned up a little. And when you finish, why don't you call Captain Hamilton and tell him I want to be put in a safe house. Just me, by myself. Then you won't have to worry about me and what I think is important."

Cody gazed at her pensively. "And what is it you think is important, counselor?"

Dana looked at the man she'd loved. How had she painted herself into this corner? How could she explain to him what was missing in her life, what had been missing in their life together? "Well, for some people, there's more to life than trying to save the world alone. To some people, what's important is home and f-family." She frowned as the familiar ache began in her chest. She glanced at Cody, who looked stricken.

Shaking her head, she turned away. She didn't want to get into this discussion. Sipping her coffee casually, she waved her hand. "Go take your shower. Maybe it will cool you off some."

For a moment, Cody was silent behind her. Then he drew an exasperated breath. "Fine." He left the kitchen.

Why did they always end up hurting each other? She regretted her last words. It was playing dirty, to mention family. Somehow, the two of them had made a silent agreement not to mention the baby they'd lost, and now she'd brought it up twice. Her heart felt as if it was ripping in two. If only...

Famous last words. *If only.*

If only Cody could have been happy just being a regular cop, maybe their marriage could have worked. If only his biggest worry each day had been how many traffic tickets he'd given out. If only he weren't a homicide detective.

Oh, he'd had job offers. He probably still did. He was a good cop. He was intelligent, obviously management material. There had been a time they'd talked about moving to a small, quiet community and raising a family. There had been a time when they talked about their hopes and dreams, a time when being in love had been enough.

A memory blindsided her. They'd spent their honeymoon here at the lake house, unable to afford to go anywhere else. Cody had somehow gotten a bottle of champagne and caught a bucketful of crawfish, and they'd sat at this table and popped the mud bugs open and sucked their heads and pulled the tender meat out of the shells with their teeth. It was exciting and spontaneous and one of the most wonderful days of her life.

She shivered. How incredibly erotic eating crawfish had been. And how typically Cody.

Champagne and crawfish and fresh new love. Love that hadn't had time to be tarnished by anger and fear and pain.

She heard the pipes screech as Cody turned on the shower. She roused herself from useless, sentimental memories.

While he was showering, she'd better get the bed made and fix something for breakfast if they were going to leave this morning. She smoothed the sheets, feeling a faint, lingering warmth where Cody had lain.

I came in to check on you, he'd said. She picked up his pillow and buried her face in it. It smelled like him, kind of wild and faintly sweet and musky. Tears pricked her eyes.

She'd hoped she'd never have to see him again. Seeing him only brought back all the pain she'd suffered, pain she'd sworn she would never allow herself to feel again. She couldn't take it.

She would never love anyone the way she'd loved Cody. She would never invest her heart, her soul, in anything the way she had in the baby they'd created together, then lost.

In the shower, she heard Cody moving around, dropping the soap, banging his elbows against the sides of the fiberglass enclosure that was too small for his tall frame. She heard him mutter a curse, and a small, unwilling smile curved her lips. They'd showered together in that tiny space, she remembered. Showered and done other, more interesting things.

How had they fit in there? How had they ever fit together?

Stop it! She pummeled the pillow as if it were her brain, and she could knock the memories out of it. Glancing at the bathroom door, she suddenly had a vision of Cody walking out into the bedroom stark naked, his body glistening with drops of water, his hair wet and slicked back. It would be just like him.

She had to get out of here before he came out. She tossed the pillow onto the bed and quickly smoothed the bedspread just as she heard Cody curse loudly and turn the water off.

She headed toward the door to the living room but

a huge crash stopped her. She turned around and listened.

Cody cursed again, this time more loudly and more colorfully. She smothered a laugh at the diversity and uniqueness of his language, even as she wondered if he'd somehow hurt himself.

"Cody?" she called out tentatively, moving toward the bathroom door. "Are you all right?"

The door burst open and Cody stood framed in the doorway, a towel slung precariously around his hips and his hair full of dripping, bubbling shampoo.

Chapter Seven

Dana tried to compose her face, but the sight of Cody standing there, so masculine and sexy, his body glistening with water, his hair white with soap and spiked in a dozen different directions above his furious face, was hilarious. She burst out laughing.

"What are—you doing?" she managed to say through the laughter.

He glared at her, his electric-blue eyes and ominous expression only adding to the caricature of dangerous, dauntless cop *en déshabillé* with shampoo running down his neck and chest.

"My damn arm hurts too much to wash my damn hair!" he shouted, dashing suds out of his eyes and squinting.

She put her hand over her mouth and tried not to laugh out loud.

"I'm glad you find this so amusing," he growled, grabbing at the towel as it came close to slipping down over his lean hips. "Do you think you could stop laughing long enough to hand me my jeans?"

Dana was thoroughly enjoying herself. She couldn't remember the last time she'd laughed—really laughed.

It had probably been with Cody, she thought with a slight twinge of regret.

Sobering a little as a result of her thoughts, she tossed a pair of jeans at him and grinned when he fumbled to catch them and hold the towel up at the same time.

"If you can get your jeans on by yourself, come out on the deck and I'll rinse your hair with the garden hose." She left, resolutely closing the bedroom door behind her, quelling a sudden urge to help Cody into his jeans.

She wiped her eyes as she stepped out onto the deck and turned on the water spigot, then traced the tangled hose to the spout.

She adjusted the water pressure to a steady stream that would do for rinsing hair, then opened up one of the vinyl chairs stacked against the deck railing, eyeing it carefully, looking for bugs or spiders.

As she was hosing off the chair, Cody stepped out onto the deck, a towel around his neck and his hair smoothed back, though still coated in shampoo.

"The chair's wet," he grumbled.

Dana shrugged. "There were bugs on it. Do you want your hair rinsed or not?"

"This is my only clean pair of jeans."

Laughter bubbled up in Dana's chest, making her feel bold and a little reckless. "So take them off," she said gaily.

Cody glared at her, but she spotted a glimmer in his eyes. "It would serve you right if I did."

She cocked her head and grinned. "Your choice, sir. I'm just the shampoo girl."

A reluctant smile tugged at his mouth and Dana's heart flipped. He was so handsome when he smiled.

He had the face of an angel when he smiled, he looked like the devil himself when he grinned, and his face turned fierce and demonic when he was angry.

"Okay," he sighed. "Just get it over with and try not to soak me, please."

"Can you lean your head back?"

"Yes, I can lean my head back." He gazed up at her, amusement intensifying the blue of his gaze.

"Damn it, Cody," she muttered as she ran her fingers through his sudsy hair, tracing the shape of his head with her hands. "It's going to take forever to rinse all this out. Did you use half a bottle of shampoo?"

"Why, was that too much?"

She sniffed in disgust. He was serious. "Men!" she exclaimed. "You have no clue. How do men ever get along without a woman? You always did use too much shampoo. I was forever buying more."

"Yeah," he responded. "More of that rosy stuff you washed your hair in. You never bought enough of mine. Do you know how many times I had to arrest someone with my hair smelling like roses?"

Dana chuckled at the vision his words evoked. "It served you right. It's wasteful to use this much shampoo. Look at your hair, it's going to take a half hour to get it all rinsed out. Turn your head."

He didn't move.

"Cody, turn your head."

She leaned over to run water on the other side of his head, and suddenly realized her breasts were pressed against his cheek, and his breath warmed her skin through her T-shirt. She shivered, while her insides tightened and her breasts ached. A fierce longing swept through her, speeding up her heart.

He took a long breath. "Mmm, you smell like roses all over," he whispered against the skin of her breast. "I'd forgotten you smell like roses everywhere."

His mouth brushed her cloth-covered nipple and she gasped. She jerked back, and when she did, the stream of water caught Cody square in his face.

"Hey!" he shouted, coming up out of the chair in one swift fluid motion.

Dana jumped backward. "What?" She recoiled, her knees like jelly from reaction.

"What do you mean, what? You sprayed water in my face, that's what." He grinned devilishly and started advancing on her.

She held the water hose in front of her like a weapon. "Cody," she warned. "Sit down. You still have shampoo in your hair." She inched backward, brandishing the hose. "I'm warning you, Cody. One more step and I'll—"

She never got to finish her threat, because he lunged at her, grabbing the hose. She hung on as long as she could, which was about one half of a second. Then he wrested the hose from her hands and she had no choice but to run to the other side of the deck.

Her heart hammered frantically, in excitement and anticipation. "Cody…!"

He grinned and pointed the hose so a stream of water splashed just in front of her feet.

"Cody, you'll hurt your arm." Despite the prospect of being soaked, Dana was surprised to find she was thoroughly enjoying herself. It was incredible how all her careful planning, her structured, ordered life, could fall completely and delightfully apart when her ex-husband acted like an adolescent. She bit her lip, forcing herself to look stern. She held up one hand. "Don't you dare get me wet, Cody. I'll—"

"What?" he asked innocently, his voice at odds with his devilish grin. He kept coming toward her. "You'll what? Sue me? Serve me with a summons? Tell me, counselor. What will you do?" He took another step forward and pointed the hose so the water splashed on her bare toes.

She tried to back up again, but the deck rail stopped her. "Cody!" she squealed, and made a desperate lunge for the hose.

He turned it full on her, and water gushed over her breasts and belly and down her legs. She held out her hands toward the spout, but that only spread the spray so that her face and hair got soaked, too. "Cody!" she squealed. "Stop it!"

Cody was laughing out loud, and despite herself, Dana was laughing too. Laughing and playing and feeling like a kid, like she had when they'd first gotten married and Cody had been able to turn anything into a delightful, sexy game.

He relaxed, and she saw her chance and took it. She grabbed the hose and managed to turn it back onto him for an instant before he overpowered her again. They struggled together with the water hose between them, both of them drenched and fast becoming weak with laughter.

Finally, with a grimace of pain, Cody let the hose drop to the deck floor. Dana was still pressed back against the rail and Cody leaned against it, too, and put his good arm around her, still laughing.

She wiped her face and pushed her wet hair back. The early morning air was cool and she shivered a little, then realized Cody was holding her close, and he had become quiet and still.

They were both dripping wet. Dana felt the odd sensation of Cody's skin against hers—cool on the surface and warm underneath. It stirred memories.

Suddenly, everything stirred memories inside her, unwanted memories, happy, erotic memories of showering together, of making love in the cool waters of the lake with Cody holding her up until they both sank beneath the water as passion overwhelmed them.

He laid his chin briefly on top of her head, and she realized just how flimsy wet cotton could be. She was embarrassingly aware of her body, covered only by the soaked T-shirt and shorts. A quick glance told her that her breasts were clearly outlined by the wet cotton, her nipples puckered, more obviously erect through the wet white material than if she'd been naked.

She strained against Cody's hold and looked up at him. His gaze traveled from her face down to her breasts, and through his wet jeans she felt the heat and hardness of him. He was becoming aroused. The awful thing was that her brain, in triggering those memories, had caused her own body to echo the reaction of his.

Through the endless sleepless nights since their divorce, she had yearned for the comfort of his long, warm body, and the closeness they'd once shared. She'd craved the feel of him filling her, coaxing her to ecstasy. There had been nights when she'd thought she would die from the loneliness. Moments when she would have borne anything, even the uncertainty of his job, if he would just hold her in the nighttime and make her laugh through the day.

For an instant she leaned into his embrace, unable

to stop herself, like an alcoholic sneaking just one swallow of liquor, just one drink.

"Chère?" His voice was questioning as his hand ran up her back to her neck and he wrapped his fingers around her nape, his thumb tracing her jaw. She lifted her head, caught in a dream of her own making, believing that she could have just this one embrace, just one kiss, and then go back to her orderly life without a regret.

His mouth touched hers, the taste and the feel so familiar, so welcome, it made her want to cry.

"Cody, I don't know if…" A sweet, intense ache started deep inside her as his mouth covered hers, cool yet warm, like his skin. He held her head immobile as his tongue scraped gently against her teeth. She yielded, and felt him harden against her.

He lifted his head slightly, his blue eyes intense and passionate. He touched her mouth with his thumb. "Ah, *chère,* you're just as gorgeous as you ever were."

"Oh, sure," she murmured.

"You never have believed me, have you? Your mirror doesn't tell you how green your eyes are?" He kissed her eyelids softly. "Admirers don't praise the curve of your cheek?" His mouth trailed a line of fire down her cheekbone. "Perfect strangers don't whistle as you walk down the street?" He nibbled on her earlobe, as his hand crept up under the wet material of her T-shirt to skim the underside of her breast.

"Cody," she breathed raggedly, "what are you doing?"

"Trying to show you how gorgeous you are." His thumb grazed the tip of her breast and liquid heat pooled in her lower abdomen.

She shivered. "I'm not sure we should do this."

His mouth came back to hers and he kissed her again, stealing her breath, stealing her will.

"What should we be doing, then?" he muttered, his breath warm on her lips. "Arguing about the best way to keep you alive?"

His words stripped away the haze of passion that fogged her brain. She remembered the danger that was a part of him, and fear streaked through her like lightning.

She pulled away.

"Chère?" Cody held on to her briefly, but she folded her arms across her chest and turned her back to him, hiding her face as well as her body from his gaze until she could get her ragged breathing under control.

She squeezed her eyes shut and took a long breath. "Well, now we're both soaked."

Behind her, he stiffened. "Yep. Soaked," he said, his voice tinged with bitterness.

She went over and turned off the water, then gathered her courage and faced him. "I guess I'll shower, now that I'm all wet, and then you can make that phone call. I really think it's a mistake for us to be here together."

"Sure. You shower. I'll make the phone call." He nodded, his face blank.

She knew she'd hurt him. It seemed as if that was what she was best at. "Cody, I'm…"

He nodded shortly. "I know. Go take your shower."

CODY STARED OUT TOWARD the lake. There were still a few wisps of fog that hadn't been burned off by the sun yet, and they made the scene look unreal, like a fantasy. But the situation he was in was real. Too real.

He'd thought he'd gotten over his ex-wife. He'd thought he was doing okay. After all, he had his job. And that was what really mattered. He was a cop. He couldn't change that. It had cost him his marriage, cost him a chance at fatherhood, but he'd thought he'd come to terms with all that.

But convincing himself he was over Dana while he filled up his time with work, and remaining convinced when she was standing right in front of him, her body slick with water, her clothes clinging to all the wonderful, sexy parts of her, were two totally different things.

His heart ached at the echo of her infectious laugh, that laugh he'd been able to coax from her all too seldom in the last months of their marriage.

But she'd laughed this morning. She'd laughed and he'd felt his heart filling up with her again.

He loved the way she'd gotten caught up in their game. For a few moments, she'd let her guard down enough to let him in, to respond to him. He felt it in the way her lips parted, in the slow, reluctant relaxation of her body against him. He heard it in the tiny gasp she'd uttered as his mouth came down on hers.

Cody groaned as his body reacted to his thoughts. He shook his head angrily. He balled his hand into a fist and slammed it down on the railing.

Not again! He couldn't get hung up on Dana again. He'd been doing fine, as long as he hadn't had to see her.

Why couldn't he keep his hands off her? It shouldn't be that hard. She'd certainly always managed easily enough. He envied the way she could turn on and off like the water spigot.

As soon as he'd stepped across her invisible line, she'd turned off. It was something she was very good at.

He'd always considered it a personal triumph when he could get past her point of no return, that point beyond which she could no longer resist him. It had delighted him each and every time he'd coaxed from her the uninhibited passion he knew was inside her.

For a while, after they were married, he'd almost managed to destroy it, that impenetrable armor she kept around her heart. But something happened, something that caused her to pull back just a little, and afterward, it had gotten harder and harder to coax her over it, to tempt her into letting down her guard completely.

It was as if she was protecting herself from him.

He ran his fingers through his wet hair. Thinking about the past was getting him nowhere. He needed to call the station, find out what was going on. Sitting here like a bump on a log while somebody else took care of his problem was not his style. He went inside and got his cell phone and dialed the precinct.

"Hey, Olsen. It's Maxwell. Detective Gautier around?"

"Detective Maxwell. How's your arm, sir?"

"Just fine."

"Well, I just want you to know we're doing all we can here."

Cody cursed under his breath. "Meaning, you haven't got a lead on Fontenot yet?"

"Uh, no sir. I should let you talk to Captain Hamilton."

"Where's Dev?"

"I'm not sure, sir. Let me put you through to the captain."

Cody slapped his palm down on the table and dropped into a chair. Obviously, nobody had managed to track down the bastard. He had to get back there.

Dana heard Cody talking on the phone when she came out of the shower. She pulled on a pair of white jeans and a sleeveless top and ran a comb through her wet hair, all the time trying to hear what Cody was saying and piece together the whole conversation.

She heard the word *Pensacola* and her pulse began to pound. Was Angie okay? She walked into the living room just as he turned off the phone.

"Well?" she said, hands on hips, heart in her throat. "What was all that about Pensacola? Every one of you promised me my sister would be okay. She is, isn't she?"

"She's just fine." Cody stood up. "That was Captain Hamilton. Dev checked out the agency where Fontenot rented the car. He paid cash, but you have to give them a certain amount of information or they won't rent you a car. For insurance purposes."

Dana sighed. "I know that. So what about the rental car?"

"Well, we knew he asked the attendant for a map of Pensacola. But nobody's been able to spot the car." Cody wiped his face and Dana noticed how pale he was.

"Cody? Are you sure about Angie?" She grabbed Cody's arm. "Did he go to Pensacola or not? What about the kids?" Her sister had two children, a girl and a boy, whom she was rearing alone after her husband had been killed in an offshore drilling accident.

"I told you, they're okay. The Pensacola police have been alerted."

Dana's heart pounded with fear. "Oh, that's comforting. More police. Damn it, Cody. I don't want my family involved in all this. Why haven't they caught him? And what are they going to do about protecting Angie and Ben and Chrissy?" She paced back and forth across the little living room.

"Angie and the kids are already on their way to a safe house. Fontenot has one thing on his mind. Getting me. As soon as he realizes we're not there, he'll be back on our trail." He stared at the phone as if it would give him some answers. "If he really went there at all," he muttered.

Dana didn't like the look of worry on his face. "What is it, Cody? Why are you so worried? If they've got the rental car license, why can't they just arrest him?"

Cody looked up at her. "In the first place, like I told you, nobody's seen the car. And in the second place, think about it. He hasn't done anything."

"Not done anything? He rigged a gun that almost killed you in your own apartment. He broke into my condo and stole my earring. He tampered with my car."

"I can't prove that was Fontenot. The gun was untraceable. I've told you before, the man's diabolical. That's the problem. He's too clever to think we'd go to your sister's. And he's too smart to let the police trace him through a rental car. I don't like it. There's something I'm missing."

Dana shivered. "You're scaring me. You act like this man is some kind of evil genius or something."

Cody threw the phone onto the couch. "You just

refuse to believe anything I say, don't you? Don't you remember what he did? Fontenot knew his wife had a heart condition. He knew she was terrified of snakes.'' His laser-sharp gaze riveted her where she stood. ''He hung a dead cat over her bed, while she was asleep, its blood dripping on the pillow right beside her head. She didn't wake up until she felt the sticky wetness of the blood on the pillow.''

''Oh, Cody. Don't.''

''He put snakes in her refrigerator. The woman was terrified of snakes. She opened the refrigerator and the sight of all those snakes tumbling out onto the floor gave her a heart attack. He murdered her just as surely as if he'd shot her. Look at this.'' He held up his bandaged arm.

Dana glanced at him then turned her head.

He grabbed her arm and turned her back to face him. ''Look at it. It's a bullet wound. The man is playing with me. He swore when I testified against him that he'd get me.''

''I know it's a bullet wound, thank you. That's what I've been talking about. You think you're invincible. You think you're superman or something.'' Dana looked at the bandage on Cody's arm and remembered the first thing that had come into her head when she'd seen the booby trap.

Too slow.

''So if he's playing with you, why'd he rig a gun to kill you?''

''It wasn't supposed to kill me. It wasn't even supposed to hit me. It was a message. He rigged it purposely so that I would feel the pull of the cord when I opened the door. I should have heard the hammer click.''

She nodded. "Too slow. So why didn't you?"

"Why didn't I what?"

"Feel the wire? Hear the hammer click? Why did you get shot?" She regretted asking the questions as soon as they were out of her mouth, because she already knew the answer. She closed her eyes, trying to keep the tears that were burning in her throat from escaping.

When Cody spoke, his voice was soft, reluctant. "I guess I wasn't paying attention. I was thinking about something else."

Chapter Eight

Cody's words rang in her ears until she wanted to cover them with her hands.

I was thinking about something else.

"You were thinking about my earring." Her head down, her eyes closed, she didn't even realize she'd spoken aloud until after she'd finished. She'd known it when she'd seen the booby trap at his apartment. His words confirmed it.

She lifted her head and looked at him, and knew with the instinctive knowledge of lovers that he was thinking the same thing she was. They never should have gotten into this conversation. It revealed too much about both of them.

He dropped his gaze, whirled around and slammed out of the house. Dana stood in the middle of the floor staring after him for a long time after he disappeared down the deck steps.

His words echoed around her. Remorse, sharp and stinging, streaked through her. He'd almost gotten killed because he was thinking about her. The tears she'd been trying to hold back pricked her eyes.

"Oh, God." She blinked furiously and looked around, desperate for something to stop her thoughts.

Without really thinking about what she was doing, she pulled sandwich stuff and cold drinks out of the refrigerator. She couldn't dwell on what might have happened, what might still happen. She couldn't get caught up again in worrying about Cody every second of every day.

Right now she had other things to worry about. She had to worry about her sister and herself, and endure this uncertainty until the police caught Fontenot and she could get back to her normal, boring life.

She slapped meat and cheese between slices of bread and wrapped them hastily in plastic wrap. Then she grabbed a couple of oranges and stuffed them and the sandwiches and the drinks in a snack-size cooler.

After changing into a swimsuit and tossing sunscreen, bug repellent and a can of wasp spray into a bag, she stepped out into the sun and headed down to the lake the way Cody had gone.

FONTENOT LAID THE SMALL dried fish on the back seat of the rental car. It had taken him a long time to find a herring, and he wasn't pleased that it was dried. He'd have preferred it fresh.

"One makes do," he muttered as he dusted his hands together fastidiously. "One makes do." He closed the car door carefully, so the fish wouldn't be disturbed, then walked around to the back.

He eyed his artwork, and smiled. He'd done an excellent job of altering the license plate. A careful application of acrylic paint had turned the four into a one, and the *B* into an *E*. Almost undetectable at even a short distance.

After making sure no one was watching him, Fontenot crouched down and peeled the elastic, dried paint off the license plate's surface, restoring the plate to its original, recognizable numbers. A sliver of white paint caught under his fingernail. With a grimace of distaste, he flicked at it with his thumbnail until it was gone.

There, he thought. He was ready. While the stupid police were swarming over the car and trying to figure out the significance of the herring, he would finish his latest project, then drive across the lake and visit his victims. How pathetic they were, thinking he couldn't find them. The connection of Mrs. Maxwell's brother to the house on Lake Pontchartrain was ludicrously simple to trace.

He walked across the street to where the disgusting car he'd acquired sat. He retrieved his handkerchief from his pocket, then slid into the driver's seat. He pulled on his leather driving gloves before starting the engine, and laid his handkerchief on the seat beside him. He'd need it. The car was filthy.

It was too bad about the previous owner. Fontenot's mouth curled in contempt. When he'd inquired about purchasing the wreck, she had protested, claiming she could never get as reliable a car for the amount he was offering her. His fingers twitched and he licked his lips and closed his eyes. The human spinal cord was such a fragile thing. It barely took a flick of the wrist to snap it.

With a sigh, Fontenot roused himself and pulled out into traffic. He glanced at his watch. His timing was impeccable, but he couldn't afford to linger. He still had some finishing touches to put on the bomb.

CODY SAT IN THE PIROGUE, halfheartedly fishing with a cane pole and cursing at himself. He pulled the line out of the water and tossed it a little closer to the fallen tree. It was already getting hot. He should have put on a T-shirt. He'd probably be the color of a boiled crawfish by the time he felt as though he could go back up to the house and face Dana again.

What a stupid-ass thing he'd said. He'd never meant to let her know how worried he really was, but she got so damned irritating at times that he'd found himself yelling at her before he knew it.

He'd seen the realization dawn in her olive-green eyes at his words. He'd regretted them as soon as he'd said them.

I guess I wasn't paying attention. Of course he hadn't been paying attention. That bastard Fontenot had known exactly how to get to him.

Knowing that Fontenot would stop at nothing to get him was a horrible knowledge. It didn't bother him so much for himself. He was good at taking care of himself, at least when he wasn't out of his mind with worry for his wife.

What had Cody terrified was what Fontenot would do to Dana.

God, sometimes he could understand why she hated the life he lived, why she hadn't been able to bear the uncertainty, the constant fear that the next case might be the one that would kill him.

He'd always thought it was exhilarating, living on the edge. He'd loved the excitement, the danger. But now the danger was too close to Dana, and suddenly her normal boring life was beginning to look pretty good to him.

He wiped sweat off his forehead. It was his fault. His fault that she had to be here, hiding out with him. His fault her safe, orderly life was disrupted. His fault that a maniac was trying to kill him and wouldn't hesitate to kill her to get to him.

He glanced around, checking out the area as he'd done every few hours since they'd arrived. Just like every time before, the inlet was quiet, peaceful...safe. Even though he knew Dev and the guys were tracking Fontenot's movement, he thought it was too quiet.

He lifted the pole and repositioned the line. He couldn't stand it here much longer. The inactivity chafed at him. He itched to be in the thick of things. He'd give anything to be the one to catch Fontenot. His pulse sped up at the prospect, then he remembered what Dana had said.

This isn't some cops-and-robbers game, Cody. That isn't make-believe blood.

Yes, he'd give almost anything to catch Fontenot. But what if he had to give up Dana again? What if he had to choose between another chance at loving her and his job? He didn't want to think about the answer to that question.

Sometimes he hated his job. It was his job that had cost him his marriage. Would it cost Dana her life?

He pushed his fingers through his hair, wishing he could push out the disturbing thoughts with them. Pulling the line out of the water, he cast it toward another likely spot where a catfish might be hiding.

"So now what?"

He stiffened. He hadn't heard her come up behind him. He was sitting with his back to the house and she'd come all the way down the hill without him hearing her. *Not very professional, Detective.*

Her voice was small and, if he weren't mistaken, apologetic. A twinge of regret stung the back of his throat. He didn't want an apology from her. He didn't want her to think it was her fault he'd gotten shot.

He turned his head slightly, until he could see her out of the corner of his eye. "Now what, what?" he asked gently.

"What are we going to do now? Stay here?" she replied.

He twisted enough to get a good look at her. She had on a tiny swimsuit and a cover-up made of some kind of loose woven stuff that didn't really cover up anything. He swallowed.

"Yep. The captain advised me to keep you here for another day or so."

"Here." She took off her sandals and tossed them into the pirogue and threw a bag of stuff in on top of them. "Is the boat safe? There's some wasp spray in the bag there."

"Wasp spray?" He rolled his eyes. "Did the Boy Scouts come to you when they needed a motto? Sunscreen would have been a better idea."

"Very funny." She stuck her tongue out at him and stepped into the boat, balancing herself with the little cooler.

Cody took the cooler and held out his hand to her. She took it, but only long enough to get herself seated.

"Careful," he said, eyeing the edge of the pirogue that was pulled up onto the bank. "Don't knock the boat loose. I don't want to drift away from the bank."

She glared at him. "I've climbed in and out of pirogues all my life, thank you. There's sunscreen in there, too."

"Of course there is. How *do* you manage to always be so damned prepared?" he asked. "Do you carry sunscreen and moist towelettes and a little bitty bathing suit with you everywhere you go, just in case you might have a chance to sunbathe while hiding out from desperate criminals?'' He pulled a package of Wet Wipes out of her bag of stuff and held it up, managing to look amused and irritated at the same time.

"No," she said icily, wondering how her effort to be nice to him had ended up in another argument. "As I've told you about four thousand times, I was planning to come up here this weekend. I was already packed."

"Ah, well, that explains it. You planned it. Of course."

"Speaking of planning, you should have a T-shirt on," she said, before he could make another smart-ass remark about her plans. "You know how easily you sunburn."

"Why didn't you plan to bring me one?" he threw back at her.

"You're mean, Cody. Mean and nasty."

"Fine." He turned his back to her.

"So how long do we have to stay here? A day? Two?"

Cody shrugged. As he lifted the cane pole and swung the line a little closer to the fallen tree, Dana watched the muscles play sinuously across his back. She hadn't forgotten the feel of them under her hands as he'd moved above her long ago, in another lifetime, when they were lovers.

How could mere flesh and bone stir such erotic memories?

She blinked and turned her gaze to the cane pole he was holding. "What are you fishing for?"

He shrugged again. Damn him. She was trying to make up for their argument earlier and he was refusing to talk to her. "Talk to me, Cody. What are you using for bait?"

He sent a baleful glance her way. "Nothing."

"Nothing?" she tried to quell a chuckle, but it bubbled up, anyway. "You're expecting the fish to jump on your hook?"

His mouth quirked up reluctantly. "I didn't *plan* to do any fishing."

Her smile faded to a frown. He was still digging at her about the way she lived her life. "That's your problem, Cody. You didn't bring a T-shirt. You didn't bring bait. You don't plan anything."

She could have bitten her tongue. Why was she so touchy? What was the matter with her? She'd walked down here expressly to be nice, and she was already snapping at him.

It was just nerves. Nerves and worry. After all, they were hiding out here together because their lives were in danger. Didn't she have a right to be nervous?

"No, Dana. That's your problem, not mine. I do just fine. I like living life as it comes instead of always trying to plan what's coming next. That takes all the fun out of it." His mouth set grimly, the reluctant humor of a moment before gone.

"Why'd you come out here? I was hoping for a little peace and quiet." Despite his expression, he didn't sound resentful, just resigned.

She felt like a dark cloud, raining on his parade. Every time he made a friendly overture she turned it off. She sighed, exasperated. No matter what she did, it was wrong. She was too keyed up. Too jumpy.

"You mean you *planned* to be out here by yourself, fishing with no bait? Should I leave?"

He pushed his fingers through his hair and repositioned his fishing pole. His movements were stiff, as if his arm hurt.

She'd never felt so mean in her life. "Cody, I'm sorry. I know you're just trying to protect me. Protect us. I'm sorry you got hurt because of me."

He gave her a disgusted look. "No problem, counselor. It's just a flesh wound. All part of the job."

Dana winced. Even if he wasn't baiting his hook, he was certainly baiting her. Well, she'd come out here to try and make up to him for the way she'd been acting, and she'd be damned if she was going to let him turn her efforts into a fight.

"I brought some sandwiches and drinks. Want some?" She tried to make her voice light.

He wiped his forehead and anchored the pole in a metal holder on the seat beside him, then turned around to face her. "Sure. I never did get any breakfast."

Dana opened the cooler and handed him a cold drink. "Me, neither." She unwrapped a sandwich for him.

He bit hungrily into the sandwich, chewed for a moment, then peeked inside the slices of bread. "There's nothing on here but meat and cheese. No mayonnaise, no mustard, nothing."

Dana moaned. "Oh, no. I forgot. I wasn't planning to bring us a picnic—what? What are you grinning at?"

Cody's grin widened around his mouthful of dry sandwich. He took a long drink of cola and wiped his mouth. "You didn't *plan* to bring us a picnic? What do you mean?" His eyes were innocently wide, but that devilish grin was still there.

Dana watched him suspiciously, her face growing

warm. "I just…you know, just threw some stuff in the cooler. All I was doing was…" She scrunched her shoulders, unsure of what to say, how to explain the urge she'd had to do something for him, something unexpected.

"Spontaneous!" he shouted. "Dana Charles Maxwell did something spontaneous! This calls for a celebration." He leaned toward her and wrapped his hand around the back of her neck.

Before she could even imagine what he was about to do, he kissed her, soundly if briefly, on the mouth.

He tasted of ham and cheese and cola, and Dana was sure that if she hadn't been sitting down, her knees would have buckled. The welcome, familiar feel of his mouth closing over hers for the second time that day, even for just those few seconds, froze her into immobility. She stared at him and realized he was staring at her, the grin still on his face but fading, into a tender, bemused expression that made her extremely uncomfortable.

She didn't know how she was going to bear it if he kept kissing her. The memories were hard enough to stand, here at the lake house where they had spent so many wonderful hours. This kissing had to stop. She would just have to be sure he didn't get another chance.

"Well," she said crisply, sitting up straight. To her chagrin, she realized that she had leaned toward him during the brief seconds while he had been kissing her. "Dry or not, I think I'll have a sandwich, too. I'm starved." She pulled an orange out of the cooler. "Want one of these?"

Cody dropped his gaze to her hand, then shook his head. "Don't try to change the subject. You've been

PLAY HARLEQUIN'S

LUCKY HEARTS
GAME

AND YOU GET

- ◆ **FREE BOOKS!**
- ◆ **A FREE GIFT!**
- ◆ **YOURS TO KEEP!**

TURN THE PAGE AND DEAL YOURSELF IN...

Play **LUCKY HEARTS** for this...

exciting FREE gift!
**This surprise mystery gift
could be yours free**

when you play **LUCKY HEARTS!**
...then continue your lucky streak
with a sweetheart of a deal!

1. Play Lucky Hearts as instructed on the opposite page.
2. Send back this card and you'll receive 2 brand-new Harlequin Intrigue® novels. These books have a cover price of $4.25 each in the U.S. and $4.99 each in Canada, but they are yours to keep absolutely free.
3. There's no catch! You're under no obligation to buy anything. We charge nothing—ZERO—for your first shipment. And you don't have to make any minimum number of purchases—not even one!
4. The fact is thousands of readers enjoy receiving their books by mail from the Harlequin Reader Service®. They enjoy the convenience of home delivery...they like getting the best new novels at discount prices, BEFORE they're available in stores...and they love their *Heart to Heart* subscriber newsletter featuring author news, horoscopes, recipes, book reviews and much more!
5. We hope that after receiving your free books you'll want to remain a subscriber. But the choice is yours—to continue or cancel, any time at all! So why not take us up on our invitation, with no risk of any kind. You'll be glad you did!

© 1996 HARLEQUIN ENTERPRISES LTD. ® and ™ are
trademarks owned by Harlequin Enterprises Ltd.

Visit us online at
www.eHarlequin.com

The Harlequin Reader Service®—Here's how it works:

Accepting your 2 free books and gift places you under no obligation to buy anything. You may keep the books and gift and return the shipping statement marked "cancel." If you do not cancel, about a month later we'll send you 4 additional novels and bill you just $3.57 each in the U.S., or $3.96 each in Canada, plus 25¢ shipping & handling per book and applicable tax if any.* That's the complete price and — compared to cover prices of $4.25 each in the U.S. and $4.99 each in Canada — quite a bargain! You may cancel at any time, but if you choose to continue, every month we'll send you 4 more books, which you may either purchase at the discount price or return to us and cancel your subscription.

*Terms and prices subject to change without notice. Sales tax applicable in N.Y. Canadian residents will be charged applicable provincial taxes and GST.

BUSINESS REPLY MAIL
FIRST-CLASS MAIL   PERMIT NO. 717   BUFFALO, NY

POSTAGE WILL BE PAID BY ADDRESSEE

HARLEQUIN READER SERVICE
3010 WALDEN AVE
PO BOX 1867
BUFFALO NY 14240-9952

NO POSTAGE
NECESSARY
IF MAILED
IN THE
UNITED STATES

spontaneous two—no, three times in the past two days. You're definitely loosening up.'' He flashed his devilish grin again and took the orange.

"I have not been spontaneous!'' she responded hotly. "I've just been trying to stay alive around you.''

"Spontaneity is not a disease, *chère.* You're a lot of fun when you let yourself relax.'' He split the orange in half with his pocketknife, then peeled off sections one at a time and popped them into his mouth.

"Cody, do you have to be so sarcastic? I don't think spontaneity is a disease.'' She spoke very carefully, busying herself with her sandwich, not looking at him. "It's just that it's important to me to be in control, to know what's going to happen.'' She looked at the sandwich distastefully. She wasn't very hungry. She wrapped the uneaten portion in the plastic wrap.

"Wait. You can throw the sandwich overboard and feed the fish,'' Cody said, reaching for it. "Better yet, I can use the ham for bait.'' He peeled the bread off and tossed it overboard and rolled the ham up and threaded it onto his hook.

"Cody, I might have eaten that later.''

"Live a little, *chère,* open a fresh one.''

She glared at him but he ignored her. He tossed the line back into the water, then went back to his orange. He paused, a dripping section of fruit staining his fingers.

"Why is being in control so important?'' He popped the piece of orange in his mouth, but his gaze never left hers.

She shifted uncomfortably on the rough wooden seat of the pirogue. "I should have worn jeans,'' she grumbled. "This seat is rough and hard.''

"Dana, I asked you a question. Answer me.''

"I just don't like surprises," she said. "Please don't ever surprise me."

He shook his head. "You've said that in the past. I don't get it. There's nothing wrong with surprises. Surprises are fun. Why is it more important to you to be in control than to have fun?"

"I don't know," she snapped, confused by her reluctance to answer him. It occurred to her that there were a lot of things he didn't know about her, and a lot of things she didn't know about him.

It was kind of sad, although Dana knew it was mostly her fault. She'd never talked about herself or her past. It was a part of her need to control her world, to keep out the hurt. And it had always been easy to distract Cody. She smiled reluctantly. Usually with a kiss. This time, she answered his question with one of her own. "Why is it more important to you to get the bad guys than it is to protect yourself?"

"Protect myself? I protect myself. What are you talking about?" He looked at her oddly. "I'm very careful."

"No you're not. You keep getting shot."

"If I weren't careful, I'd keep getting killed."

She grimaced. "That's a very bad joke. If you cared about—people, you wouldn't put yourself in danger."

"Chère, I care about *people."*

His keen look told her he knew what she hadn't said. *If he cared about her.* "But my job is keeping people safe. And if that puts me in danger, well…"

He shrugged his shoulders. The unconsciously sexy movement distracted Dana. His golden skin shone, faintly pink where the sun had kissed it. His elbows rested on his knees and his fingers were covered with juice as he slowly peeled the orange.

Pulling her thoughts back to what he'd said, Dana shook her head. "I just don't understand your logic. Of course you care. It's who you are. You care about keeping all people safe. Everywhere. But you have this idea that you can save the whole world, when all I want is…" She stopped.

"When all you want is what, *chère?*"

She couldn't tell him what she'd been about to say. It sounded selfish. *All I want is you, safe, with me.*

She wiped her hands on a paper napkin and spread it across one knee, then folded it carefully, smoothing the edges over and over. "I just want a safe, normal life. You know, the usual. Someone who understands their responsibilities. When someone cares about someone, they have a responsibility, and…"

"And what, Dana? What are we talking about here?"

She smoothed the napkin. "Nothing."

"Then why are you so upset?"

She glanced up at him to find him watching her with a curious expression on his face. "I'm not upset. What do you mean?"

"Look at what you're doing, *chère.*"

"What am I doing?"

"The way you're folding that napkin. Like the world will end if you don't get every corner folded just perfect." A shadow crossed his face for an instant and he grabbed the paper napkin out of her fingers.

"Wad it up and throw it away, for God's sake!" He ripped it in two and tossed it into the lake, shaking his hand when the flimsy paper stuck to his orange-juice-covered fingers.

"Cody, that's littering."

"Dana, it's biodegradable."

"See. That's what your problem is. You're so—intense."

He laughed wryly. "It's a defense mechanism against your obsessiveness."

She winced. "Please try not to make everything I say into some kind of joke. I'm serious. You attack everything like you're afraid you'll miss one second of life. It's exhausting. It's scary."

"What do you mean, scary?"

She swallowed. Had she really said scary? "Hey," she said, laughing uncomfortably, "why the third degree? I feel like you're cross-examining me."

He was getting to her and he knew it. He'd always been able to do that. It was funny that she was the lawyer but he was the one who could fire off uncomfortable questions like a member of the Dream Team.

"Maybe I am, counselor."

"Don't call me that. You make it sound like an insult. I'm a good lawyer."

"You were a good public defender." His brow wrinkled for a second as he peeled off another section of orange.

"That was too intense, too."

"Don't you think intense is better than boring?"

"Absolutely not. I am perfectly happy with boring."

"Now, why would you want that, *chère?* When you could have me?" Flashing his angelic smile, Cody leaned forward and pushed a dripping, sticky section of orange at her mouth.

"Cody, stop—" Dana's open mouth was suddenly full of sweet succulent orange and two of Cody's fingers. She caught his wrist reflexively, but he didn't pull away. Instead, he brushed his fingertips across her teeth.

Her tongue touched them. She didn't mean to, it was an instinctive movement, but as soon as her tongue touched his fingers, a searing thrill ripped through her belly, knocking all thoughts of logic or boredom out of her head.

Cody took a swift breath and leaned closer to her.

She saw what he was going to do, and every brain cell in her head screamed *Danger! Run! Don't let him kiss you!* But her heart refused to listen to her brain, and her body was acting on pure instinct.

Dazedly, she leaned forward, too, her eyes on his mouth, her mouth full of the sweetness of fruit and his fingers. As if in a dream, her lips curled around them and she sucked, her breath quickening at the erotic feel and taste of his skin against her tongue.

Then the golden halo of his head was blocking the sun and his mouth replaced his fingers. Now she tasted orange and sun and salty male sweat, and she savored it like the finest wine.

He kissed her tentatively at first, a sweet gentle touching of lips to lips, as his damp fingers trailed down the column of her throat.

Then, slowly, as if he were approaching a half-wild kitten, he knelt before her and pulled her to him and wrapped his arms around her. He kissed her like a lover kissed his love, like a husband kissed his wife. He molded her body to his, using his big, elegant hands to keep her there, skin to skin, heartbeat to heartbeat.

Carefully, as if she were afraid he'd disappear, she laid her palms against his bare chest, sliding her fingers through the sparse crisp hairs that grew there. It felt so good to touch him again, to feel his strength, to feel his steady heartbeat against her breasts.

Her head spun, her heart fluttered like a captured butterfly, and her hands crept up his naked chest to his sun-warmed shoulders. His skin was hot and smooth, its velvety surface covering the steel-hard muscles she'd always loved to trace with her palms. Once she'd known every plane, every bulge on his beloved body.

Lost in erotic fantasy, she opened her mouth fully, allowing him in. She heard him gasp. She felt his arousal spring up hard against her.

Cody whispered to her...soothing words, sexy, naughty words, the love play he'd always used to calm her shyness while he worked his magic on her body. He cupped her breast, running his thumb over her nipple beneath the thin material of her swimsuit top. Her breast ached and throbbed.

Oh, God. It had been so long, and she did love him so much.

His hand slid downward, caressing her bare belly, as her stomach muscles contracted in anticipation. His fingers tantalized her as his hand reached around to cup her bottom and pull her closer, closer.

Dana's whole body pulsed with yearning. It felt so right, and so familiar, to be held, to be worshiped by Cody. No one had ever made her feel so special and beautiful.

It was all she'd ever dreamed of, and everything she'd always feared. She was about to be lost, overwhelmed by his intensity, his power, his danger.

Almost too late, Dana heard her thoughts above the pounding of her heart.

Danger.

Chapter Nine

She pushed away, flattening her palms against his chest, turning her head aside, using all of the will she possessed to drag her mouth away from his.

He let her retreat, but only a few inches. He still held her imprisoned in his arms, his head was still bent toward her, proving to her that he could still be kissing her if he wanted to, telling her she was powerless against his greater strength.

"Come on, *chère*," he whispered. "Relax. We're out here in the sun, nobody around for miles. You and me and the gators. That's all."

He smiled sweetly and Dana almost smiled back at him, but the voice in her head wouldn't shut up. *Danger, danger!*

"Cody, don't," she said weakly, her traitorous body still yearning for him.

He obviously felt her give in, because he pulled her back against him. He was fully aroused, his hardness pressing against her insistently, with a promise she knew he could fulfill.

His blue eyes were dilated, his cheeks faintly red with passion, his male nipples erect under her palms.

"Why not, *chère?*" he whispered, his breath tickling her ear. "Live a little." He touched her earlobe with his tongue and a spear of desire stabbed her, so strong it made her moan.

"That's it, let go. Be spontaneous."

She felt passion heat her own face, felt her body respond with liquid warmth. Just touching him, just having his hands on her was like an aphrodisiac.

She gasped and buried her nose in his warm sweet hair. "This isn't a good idea," she panted as her body melted against his in languid defeat. Her breasts were taut and sore, rubbing against his chest through the thin material of her swimsuit. Her belly was rigid with expectation.

She was on fire for him. Languid heat suffused her as Cody nuzzled her neck and nibbled on her ear.

"Cody, please," she whimpered, "you're taking—advantage of me."

He chuckled and the ripple of his diaphragm sent delicious shivers through her. "Oh yes, ma'am. I most certainly am."

He ran his palm up her hip, across her bare stomach to the underside of her breast and curled his fingers around it again, intensifying the yearning inside her.

She gasped.

He turned his head and slanted his mouth over hers, stealing what was left of her breath and sending flames of desire through her again.

Her body opened to him, and warm dampness told her she was ready. Soon, if he continued, it would tell him.

His hand left her breast and moved lower, to the thin band of her bikini bottom. He slid his fingers beneath the material, caressing her belly, gently pushing lower and lower.

Dana's desire-fogged brain finally registered what was about to happen. Stiffening, she tried to make her body obey her brain, tried to withdraw from Cody's sensual seduction. She pushed against his chest.

He sighed raggedly and pulled back enough to look at her.

Dana stared up at him, unable to speak through lips swollen from his kisses.

"Ah, now, don't stop." He rubbed his thumb across her nipple and she shivered. "You're so warm and sweet and sexy. We still fit together, don't we?" He smiled, a lazy, sexy smile and dipped his head to kiss her. "Relax, *chère,*" he whispered against her mouth.

No. Almost against her will Dana squeezed her eyes shut and pushed him away. She'd give anything to be able to let go, to give Cody what he wanted. *To take what she wanted.*

But getting back into the habit of being loved by Cody would only bring her pain, just like before. He was too dangerous.

"Cody, stop!" she said hoarsely, reaching as far inside her as she could for restraint, for control. With determination learned from years of disappointment, she pushed her feelings back behind the wall she kept around her heart.

"How can you possibly relax?" she asked, determinedly reminding herself of why they were at the lake house together in the first place. "There's a maniac who wants to kill you. How can you even think about—other stuff?" She strained against his embrace and finally his smile faded and he let her go.

"Sorry, counselor." He pushed away from her and sat on the pirogue seat. "I guess I forgot for an instant who I was with. For a minute there you reminded me of the gorgeous woman I married. For a minute it seemed like old times.''

''Don't do this to me, Cody.'' She looked down and pretended to be searching for her sandals, so he wouldn't notice the tears that pricked her eyes.

Stop it. He knows how to get to you. Don't let him. She swallowed hard. ''Don't try to make this weekend into some kind of reconciliation. I'm not the same person you married.''

''That's funny, 'cause I could swear you look just like her. Hardly aged at all.'' He put his finger under her chin and tilted her head up.

She resisted, desperately afraid she'd give in if she looked into his smoky, sparkling eyes.

''You are not funny.'' She swatted at his hand, then groped for her sandals. Her fingers closed around them, and she slipped them on.

''Chère?'' His finger touched her cheek, and she recoiled again.

''Don't, Cody. Please just don't.'' Her gaze met his, and she saw the pain etched in the new lines on his face.

She really hated herself. The words just spewed out, like paper through a shredder. Destroying. It seemed that was all she was good at. How could she love him so much and at the same time be so deathly afraid of giving in to him?

She stood up and started to get out of the pirogue, and almost fell. ''Ack!''

The boat was no longer pulled up on the bank, but was floating away from it.

''Damn it, Dana, sit down!'' Cody shouted, grabbing her arm. She fell back onto the hard seat.

Cody glowered at her. ''You pull the damnedest

stunts for a woman who says she plans everything. You almost fell out of the boat.''

''Well who let it drift away from shore?''

''I didn't practically turn it over getting in, you did. You dislodged it.''

''I did not.'' Dana welcomed the cleansing anger that washed the haze of desire from her brain. She wasn't being fair, but then neither was he.

They both knew perfectly well what had happened.

It frightened Dana that she'd been so overcome with plain old lust that she hadn't noticed the boat drifting away from shore. It was strangely thrilling to her, in a very scary way, that Cody hadn't noticed, either.

Her face flamed as she thought about what they had almost done in the open Cajun canoe in the middle of the day, even if it was in a secluded inlet. She stole a glance at Cody and found him watching her, a pensive frown on his face.

''What?'' She could have bitten her tongue. She didn't want to know what he was thinking.

He shook his head distractedly. ''Nothing.'' His voice was distracted, too, and his sharp blue eyes still watched her.

She swallowed. ''Well, stop looking at me that way.'' She patted the material of her swim bra, making sure Cody's questing fingers hadn't left her exposed.

''What happened just now?''

''You mean when I stood up?''

He shook his head and pushed his fingers through his hair. ''No, before. What happened?''

She spread her fingers over her chest, where her heart was beginning to pound. ''You got carried away?'' Her voice made it sound like a question. She cleared her throat.

"You got carried away," she repeated, avoiding his eyes.

"I got carried away." His face held a look of exasperation. "So what do you call what you did?"

"Me?"

"Yeah. You."

"I, um, well…"

"Would it be safe to say that you got carried away, too?"

She felt heat flood her face. "I suppose you could say that. I mean, it's not like…"

He raised his brows. "Not like what?"

It's not like I care about you. The words stuck in her throat, because she knew they weren't true. She shook her head, a little jerkily. "Don't, Cody."

"Don't what? Don't ask you uncomfortable questions? Don't talk about us, because you can't handle it?"

"Could you take me back, please?" she asked icily. "I'll leave you to some peace and quiet."

"Too late now," he said tersely as he retrieved an oar from the bottom of the boat and guided the pirogue in toward the bank.

As soon as Dana could see the bottom she jumped out of the boat and escaped up the hill toward the house. He was getting too close. Way too close. She would just have to be more careful.

Her brain lectured her in time with her swift strides. How, after all this time, could she still melt in his arms? How, after all the pain, all the heartache, could his kiss call up the good times, the exquisite memories of the once-in-a-lifetime love they'd shared so long ago?

She'd almost given in, and she knew how dangerous

that was. If she gave in to him now, she'd have to get over him all over again. And if she were truthful, she wasn't sure she had the strength.

CODY CURSED AND THREW the oar down into the boat. What an ass he was. Getting all hot and bothered about his ex-wife. He could imagine what Dev and the other guys would say. Well, the other guys, anyway. For some reason, Dev thought that Cody and Dana getting back together was the best idea in the world.

No way, he thought. Just look at her. She hadn't changed a bit. She was still much too uptight for him. Two years of marriage had taught him that. And nothing he'd seen in the past two days told him any different.

But oh, could she turn him on.

Taking her into his arms was like coming home. Kissing her had always been like nothing he'd ever felt before or, he was sure, would ever feel again. He brushed an unsteady hand over his face. He was awed at how easily they had come together, as if it had been four days instead of four long, lonely years.

As he pulled the pirogue up onto the bank, Cody lectured himself. He couldn't let himself fall in love with her again. He couldn't risk being distracted by her nearness, by the haunting scent of roses that brought back memories of the passion they'd once shared. He was here for one reason and one reason only. He was protecting her. That was all.

And if he had anything to say about it, he wasn't going to be doing that for much longer. He was going to get someone else out here to watch her, and he was going to catch Fontenot. It would be much safer that way. For her and for him.

Cody walked out onto the ancient dock that some-one, maybe Dana's grandfather's buddy, had built de-cades before. At the end of the rickety wooden pier, he surveyed the area again, to satisfy himself that there was nothing out of the ordinary. Then he pulled a deep wire basket out of the water. He could tell by the weight of the basket that they were in luck. Dozens of crawfish were piled on each other, along with a few crabs.

He hadn't caught any fish. He smiled as he remem-bered Dana's question about bait. Not a one had jumped on his hook and begged to be caught. But they could have boiled crawfish for supper, and boiled crab for dessert.

Too bad they didn't have any champagne, he thought, as a queer ache started in his chest.

He hadn't thought about their honeymoon in a long time. They'd come up to the lake house, and eaten crawfish and drunk champagne, then made love all night.

Ah, hell. There was a good reason he hadn't thought about their honeymoon. It was because that kind of memory ate into his resolve to get over his ex-wife.

He untied the basket from the mooring and started up the hill to the house, just as rain began to fall.

He flexed his shoulders and rolled his neck. He was too tense. He needed to get away from here as soon as possible. He needed action.

More than that he needed distance from Dana. It wasn't working the way he'd thought it would. He'd thought he could take things as they came. He'd thought he was over her. Boy, was he wrong.

Tonight, he'd call Captain Hamilton. Then he could do what he'd wanted to do ever since he'd heard that

Fontenot was out of prison. He could put the man back in.

He nodded, satisfied with his decision. He was going crazy up here with nothing to do. Going crazy and pulling stupid stunts, like trying to seduce his ex-wife.

All he had to do was get through tonight.

DANA WAS LAYING a fire in the fireplace when Cody came in with the crawfish. She was crouched down, nursing a tiny flame, and Cody admired the view of her backside in tight white shorts.

She glanced up. "There's a storm coming," she said, then turned back to the fire.

"Yeah. It's already starting to rain. I got a mess of crawfish and a couple of crabs."

Dana stood, dusting her hands against each other. She had taken a shower. Her hair was still damp and her face was bare of makeup and shiny, with two pink spots in her cheeks. She looked like she had when they first got married, young and innocent and shy.

"Great," she said. "I hope there's some crawfish seasoning here. I didn't bring any."

Cody dumped the basketful of wriggling animals into the sink and ran water over them. "Remember on our honeymoon, when we had to beg some from that old codger who used to live down the hill?"

He berated himself for bringing up the very thing he was trying to forget, but Dana laughed quietly, and Cody was glad he'd said it.

"I remember what he said," she responded, standing next to him at the sink, preparing the crawfish for purging. "He said, 'It don't look to me like you two need any more spice between you.'"

She stopped abruptly and turned away. "I wonder where the big pot is?" she said quickly.

Cody understood how she felt. The air between them was electric, like the summer sky outside as the storm gathered. How could he stand to stay here even one more night, so close to her?

She found the pot and he piled the cleaned and purged crawfish into it, and filled it with water while she dug into the cabinets.

With a cry of triumph she held up an ancient can of seasoning. "Voilà!"

She handed him the can, careful not to touch his fingers.

After he got the fire lit under the pot, he turned to her. "I'm going to call the captain and get somebody up here to watch you. Then tomorrow, I'm heading back to New Orleans."

Dana stared at him, her face carefully blank. "You're heading back to New Orleans. Well, that's just great."

"What's wrong with that? I figured you'd be glad to see the last of me."

A shadow crossed her face as she propped her hands on her hips. "Oh, trust me, I will be."

"Well, then, what's the problem?"

"There—is—no—problem," she ground out between clenched teeth, then turned on her heel and left the kitchen.

Cody stared after her. What was that all about? He shrugged. He was sure she was just as anxious as he was to put distance between them. But it seemed that nothing he did was right. *That was a familiar feeling.*

Getting away from here would be the best thing for him. If he thought he could risk it, he'd get her away, too. Take her to another city, to a safe house. Some-where out of Fontenot's reach. There were too many memories here, where some of their best times had been.

He stirred the crawfish with a long-handled spoon.

Maybe he shouldn't have brought up their honey-moon. They had been so young, so in love, so innocent of the problems associated with real life. He should never have mentioned it. He poured more seasoning into the pot.

DANA SAT IN FRONT of the fire, listening to the rain on the tin roof of the house, contrasting with the warm, crackling sound of wood burning. She shivered. It didn't take long for a spring rainstorm to cool things off.

She heard Cody stirring the crawfish, and shivered again, but this time it wasn't the temperature that af-fected her.

He was going back to New Orleans. He just couldn't stand not being right in the middle of the action. And obviously, he didn't want to stay here with her. It was probably for the best.

Even as the thought entered her head, an unreason-ing anger bubbled up inside her. He was going to leave her here and go off to chase the bad guy. Just like always. She picked up the poker and prodded the logs, sending sparks flying up the chimney.

"Watch it, you'll have us roasting if you poke that fire up any more."

She tossed the poker down on the hearth and stepped back. "Fine," she snapped. "You do it, then. You're so much better at everything."

''Hey, what's the matter?'' He frowned at her as he retrieved the poker and stood it back in its stand.

''Oh, nothing, Cody,'' she said shortly. ''Nothing at all, except that you haven't changed a bit. I guess you'll never change, will you?''

She sat down on the end of the sagging couch and pulled her legs up under her and crossed her arms. ''Here we are, safe and sound, and you want to go running back to New Orleans.''

Cody leaned his arms on the mantel and stared down into the fire. His shoulders were a dark reddish gold where the sun had burned him. His ribs were clearly outlined under his skin, and she could count the bumps on his spinal cord if she wanted to.

Of course, she already knew just how many and where they were, and how each one of them felt under her fingers. Disgusted with her thoughts, she dragged her gaze away from his bare back and stared into the fire.

''Dana, do you have any idea just how evil the man is?'' He closed his hands into fists against the mantel. ''Let me tell you something. I feel like I know exactly what Fontenot is thinking. I understood perfectly the message he was sending when he left your earring on my car seat. It was as clear as a typed note. You want to know what it said?''

She wanted to shake her head no, but all she could do was stare at the nape of his neck, where tense muscles bunched.

''It said *I can get to your wife. I know where she lives. I know when she's at home and when she's gone.*'' He turned and looked at her, his eyes hooded and dark. ''Do you have any idea what it did to me when I saw your earring?''

She shook her head, unable to speak around the lump of fear in her throat.

"I've never been so scared in my whole life. I was looking at a symbol of what Fontenot could do to you. He took the earring. He could have taken you." His voice broke.

"You're scaring me, Cody," she whispered, wrapping her arms more tightly around herself.

He cleared his throat. "Good. You ought to be scared. I am. Now, what do you think I should do? Sit here and wait for him?" He pushed his fingers through his hair in exasperation. "What do you want me to do, Dana?"

Dana shook her head. She knew she could never answer that question. Ever.

What she wanted him to do was hold her, comfort her, make love to her forever. And never, ever get hurt again. She wanted him to promise her that nothing bad would ever happen to either of them. She wanted him to keep her safe forever, to love her like she'd always dreamed he would.

But that was impossible. She could never tell him that, because if she did, she'd be giving up the last dregs of control she had over her heart. Then he'd know how much she needed him. And she could never allow him to know that, because, what if he didn't care?

He looked at her strangely, and she was terrified that her thoughts were clearly mapped on her face. She ducked her head and stood up.

Cody caught her arm and used his other hand to tilt her face up, so she had to look at him.

"*Chère,* are you all right?"

She pulled out of his grasp. "Of course," she retorted. "I'm just going to check on the crawfish. They're probably done by now." She turned her back on him and went into the kitchen, where the spicy smell of boiled crawfish permeated the air. It made her mouth water and jolted her with memories. She stared at the big pot helplessly.

How was she going to sit here with Cody and eat crawfish? It would be just like their honeymoon. How would they get through this evening that was a twin of the night they'd gotten drunk on champagne and crawfish and love while a summer storm raged outside?

Lost in her thoughts, Dana turned around when Cody walked into the kitchen, and his gaze caught hers. Her thoughts and memories were clearly mirrored in his blue eyes. For a long moment she couldn't move.

Then he blinked and broke the spell. He stepped toward her, and she stepped back. "Pour them into the sink and we can help ourselves," she said crisply.

They sat at the table and ate crawfish like they had six years ago on the day they got married. But this time Dana was stiff and nervous, and not hungry at all, and Cody was quiet and brooding.

After a few strained minutes, Cody cursed quietly and got up and left the room. Dana sat there for a while, picking at a mud bug, but she finally gave up and cleaned up the kitchen and put the rest of the crawfish in the refrigerator.

When she went back into the living room, the fire was blazing but Cody was nowhere around.

Chapter Ten

Dana pushed her hair back tiredly. She really couldn't blame Cody for escaping the tension in the lake house. The whole day had been a huge strain on both of them. It was amazing how many things they found to argue about for two people who hadn't seen each other in four years. It was incredible how well their bodies remembered each other. Her face burned as she thought about how easily they had come together, how naturally they had kissed, for two people who had been divorced for longer than they'd been married.

Warning herself against such thoughts, Dana went into the bedroom and got undressed. As she picked up her satin nightgown, she glanced longingly at the few clothes Cody had brought. His Police Academy T-shirt was tossed precariously on top of his duffel bag. With a quick glance over her shoulder at the bedroom door, Dana retrieved the T-shirt and slipped it on over her bare body.

She'd slept in it all this time. It was just more comfortable than her gown, she rationalized. It was comfortable and warm and familiar. *Like Cody,* her brain whispered. No, she argued with herself. It was just a T-shirt.

She got into bed and tried to sleep, but she was too keyed up. Every time she heard a sound, she tensed, wondering if it was Cody. After about fifteen minutes of tossing and turning, she got up and went into the living room.

She pulled an old quilt off the back of the couch and wrapped up in it, sitting on the floor in front of the fire. The last time they'd been here they'd made love here, on the very quilt she was wrapped in.

Dana tried halfheartedly to push the memories back behind the wall, but the storm, the fire and the quilt were in a conspiracy to make her remember, and she was too tired to fight. So she finally gave in and let her thoughts go where they would.

They had argued, like they always did, but they'd also made love, time and time again, all through that weekend. On the couch, on the floor in front of the fire, on the bed. And one of those times, they'd made a baby. Dana hugged the quilt around her and let the memories wash over her.

They had come to the lake house for a quiet weekend, to try and recapture the wonder of their first year together. They'd been happy until the first time Cody was shot. That one had been so minor it was ludicrous now, in the wake of his later, more serious wounds. But to Dana, who had never seen violence, it was a horrible nightmare.

A bullet had grazed his forearm, leaving a long bloody furrow, but no real damage. In fact, it hardly even left a scar. But Dana had panicked. It had never occurred to her that Cody could actually be shot.

Suddenly, she realized that she was the one who had always thought his job was like a television show where the good guys always win and the bad guys always go to jail, and everybody gets up at the end and goes home.

Then he'd come home with his arm bandaged and his shirt black with blood, and she had realized for the first time how much danger was inherent in his job, and how fragile his all-too-human body was.

He was just flesh and bone, breakable, mortal, and the realization scared her half to death.

So she had begun to withdraw, and she'd invested her heart in safe, mundane things. She'd started to hate her job with the public defender's office. It was much too volatile, too dangerous. She began looking for a corporate job. She lost interest in their quaint French Quarter apartment and looked at ads for apartments in the safe, quiet suburbs. And she'd tried to get him to take a desk job, or transfer to a less dangerous part of town.

They had begun to snipe at each other, and suddenly the incredible passion, the joy and the tender understanding, the balance between his intensity and her calm control, wasn't enough.

So they had come to the lake house for a weekend, to try to remember why they'd married in the first place, and she'd gotten pregnant.

They had been so excited about having a baby. Cody was more attentive, sweeter, gentler, than he'd been in a long time. He had even mentioned a job opening in Metairie, chief of detectives.

But then, he'd gotten involved in Fontenot's case. Fontenot had shot him, and Dana miscarried, and she'd had to face the fact that things hadn't really changed. They'd never change. Cody was still Cody, still diving into the heart of danger.

As long as she was married to him, she would always be afraid.

Oh, but it had been so close to wonderful. Dana blinked and realized she was crying. She couldn't remember the last time she'd really cried. Maybe never. She never allowed herself to.

To her, the most important thing was to stay in control. She was afraid if she ever let go and really, truly cried, she might never stop.

Now she didn't even know why she was crying. She had no more excuse than a little silly nostalgia, but she couldn't seem to stop the hot, unfamiliar tears.

Then suddenly, it was easier. The wall around her heart had been breached. It felt good to admit, even if it was only to herself, that she couldn't control everything all the time. So like a child, she buried her face in her hands and sobbed.

After a while, she became aware that Cody was sitting beside her. She smelled the rain and wind he'd brought in with him. She hadn't heard him come in, and he hadn't disturbed her. He just sat there quietly, not touching her.

Finally, her tears stopped. She sniffed and wiped her cheeks on the quilt.

"Feel better?" Cody settled back against the couch and put his arm around her.

Dana allowed herself to sink into his side, to appreciate his strong arm draped over her shoulders. She nodded against his chest. "I don't know what got into me," she whispered.

"It wasn't what got into you, it's what you finally let out. You carry so much around inside you. It's good to let go. I don't think I've ever seen you cry."

"I never do."

His arm tightened, pulling her closer. "Well, maybe you should. There's nothing wrong with letting go. Let someone help you. Why do you have to hold yourself so rigid all the time? Why can't you just let life flow around you?"

She stiffened at the very thought. "I can't even imagine that," she whispered. "Life is so unpredictable, so full of uncertainty. How can you just let it *flow?*"

He laughed softly, his chest rippling against her cheek. "It's easy, *chère*. You just float, like on the river, just float and let it happen. It's a good thing. Trust me."

She shook her head. "But, Cody, if you did that, then you'd just let Fontenot go, right?"

"Nope. Totally different thing. That's my job. What I'm talking about is life."

"But your life is your job."

"No. Not to me. You're the one who never could separate the two."

"You can't separate them. How can your job be separate from your life?"

"My job is what I do, not who I am."

She looked up at him. "How can you say that? Being a cop is who you are."

He pulled her back to him and pressed his face into her hair. His warm breath made her scalp tingle. "That's not so. Who I am...who I was, was your husband. Who I am now is a lonely guy who used to be married."

He chuckled. "Do you realize this is probably the most we've ever talked? I mean really talked."

Dana turned her head so her nose was pressed into Cody's chest. He was damp from the rain, and smelled clean and sweet. "How can you say that?" she protested weakly, feeling guilty, because she knew he was right.

"There's always been a part of you I couldn't reach."

"That's not true!"

"Oh, yes it is. You've never opened up to me completely."

She tried to straighten up, but he tightened his hold on her just slightly.

"*Chère,* it's okay. It's just you and me here. Just let it flow, like you used to do when we made love. You understood that, didn't you? When we couldn't do anything else, we could make love. That was one place you trusted me. Trust me now. I've just checked around outside again. There's nobody around for miles. Nobody's going to hurt you. Nobody's going to make you do anything. It's just you and me. Trust me."

Dana's heart pounded in her throat. Could she say what she'd never said to anybody? Could she explain it to him? This was Cody. This was the one person in her whole life that she'd wanted the most to trust, and she'd held that part of herself back, even from him.

She swallowed. "What do you think, Cody? That I've got some big secret that's eating me up inside?"

"Maybe."

"Well, there's nothing like that. No huge secret."

"But maybe there's a little one, eh?"

She was silent. Some part of her wanted to shrink away from him, to hide from the truth.

"Dana?"

"You'd just think it was silly."

"No, *chère.* No." He put his other arm around her

and held her close, all wrapped up in the quilt. "Trust me. There is absolutely nothing about you that I would ever think is silly."

"Not even my day planner?"

"Okay, well, your day planner."

She dug her fingers into his side and he laughed. But his words were serious. "You never told me much about yourself, you know," he whispered. "You always managed to change the subject. Usually by kissing me."

She smiled. "I learned early on how easy it was to distract you by kissing you."

"Mmm. You got that right. Never could resist your kisses."

A little thrill ran through her at his words. "It was good, wasn't it, Cody? That part of it?"

He laughed softly, the ripple of his chest sending answering ripples through her. "It was better than good. It was incredible. When you would loosen up these tight muscles and pour yourself over me like molasses, ah, *chère,* it was fantastic."

She unwrapped one hand from the quilt and threaded her fingers through the sparse hairs on his chest. He drew a swift breath and laid his hand over hers.

"No fair," he gasped as his heartbeat sped up under her fingers. "I thought you were going to answer my question."

Dana licked her lips. "It's nothing, Cody. It's just a silly notion of mine. I just like things to be consistent, that's all."

"I'd say that's the understatement of the year."

She stiffened. "See, I knew you'd laugh at me."

"No, *chère,* I'm not laughing." He continued rubbing her neck in a circular motion, and his breath quickened. "Go on. Tell me. Why is it so important for things to be consistent? Why can't you go with the flow?"

"I guess it's my father's fault," she said in a small voice. "He never stayed around much when we were kids."

Cody didn't say anything, he just entwined his fingers with hers and rubbed his thumb along her palm, as his other hand massaged her neck. After a few moments, he prodded her gently. "What about your father? You never talked much about him."

"He'd come home for a while, then he'd leave, and we wouldn't see him for months. My mother said he had a wandering heart." She started to sit up, a little embarrassed at her confession, but Cody's fingers continued to caress her neck and she relaxed back against his bare chest.

"I was the oldest. So I had to be the responsible one. He always depended on me to watch after everybody. He always promised me he'd be back."

Tears burned in the back of her throat, and somehow Cody must have known, because he pulled her closer. "It's okay, *chère*. Just keep talking. Everything's going to be fine."

She took a shaky breath, remembering. "Then one time, he left and he never came back." She closed her eyes, remembering her mother's face—resigned, frightened, heartbroken.

"You never told me that. I thought your father died."

"He did. We just didn't know about it until over a year later."

CODY CONTINUED to massage Dana's neck. He felt the tension there, the knots, the stiff muscles. His poor little Dana, waiting for her father, who didn't come home. "How old were you?"

"Twelve."

He winced. "I'm sorry. That must have been bad."

"I trusted him, you know? He promised me. He'd always come home before."

Cody's chest tightened. She'd trusted her father to come home and one time he hadn't. No wonder she couldn't bear waiting at home alone. No wonder she hated surprises.

He put a finger under her chin and lifted her face to his. "You're something, you know that?" he whispered, then he bent his head and kissed her.

Dana opened her mouth to his kiss, feeling all her resolve drain out through her fingertips against his warm, bare chest.

The thunder roared above them, nearly drowned out by the rain beating down on the tin roof. The fire crackled and spit, its light vying with the lightning that flashed around them.

Cody pushed the quilt away from her shoulders and pulled her across his lap, his kiss deepening, his arms cradling her. She wrapped her arms around his neck, pulling him closer, giving him back kiss for kiss, hardly able to breathe.

"Cody," she gasped, pushing her fingers through his hair.

"I'm here," he whispered against her mouth. "I'm right here. I won't go away, I swear. Not if you don't want me to."

He tenderly pushed her down in front of the fire and lay over her, kissing her mouth, her nose, her eyelids, running his hands down her body to the hem of the T-shirt.

Dana's brain screamed at her that this was a mistake, but she didn't listen. Right now she didn't care. Right now all she wanted to do was be careless, thoughtless, spontaneous.

She didn't want to think about what might happen tomorrow. She didn't want to worry about how she would deal with Cody after she'd let him in again. How she'd learn to live without him again. She just wanted to feel.

He slid his hand up under the T-shirt and ran his fingers up her thigh. When he discovered that she didn't have on any underwear, he took a swift breath and pulled back, smiling at her, his eyes dark with passion, his lips parted.

"Tell me you want this," he muttered. "Tell me you won't stop me. Because if you're going to stop, you'd better do it now."

She shook her head, but he grabbed her jaw.

"Tell me," he demanded.

"Don't stop," she whispered breathlessly. "Don't stop, please."

"Ah, Dana." He buried his head in the hollow of her neck, his tongue tracing patterns on her skin. "You smell like roses," he said, his voice muffled. "Always like roses."

Desire streaked through her like the lightning that streaked through the sky. She arched against him.

"Cody, please," she begged, not sure if she was begging for now or for forever. She only knew she'd missed this the past four years. She'd needed him so badly, needed his strength, his passion, his intensity.

He was the other part of her. She was only whole when she was with him.

Cody pushed his jeans off and slid the T-shirt up and over her head. He leaned up on one elbow, his gaze stripping away all the careful armor she'd spend four years building. They were both lit by firelight, their skin glowing in the flickering flames.

She watched him as he traced his hand over her collarbone, down between her breasts, down her belly. He was like a sculptor, shaping her body to suit him, touching it everywhere, leaving a trail of liquid fire where he touched.

"You are so beautiful," he whispered, and leaned down to kiss her.

Dana's heart was pounding in her throat, her body was taut with yearning, her skin was on fire for his touch. She took his face between her palms and brought his mouth down to hers.

Against his lips she whispered, "Now, Cody. Now."

He gasped raggedly, his electric-blue eyes burning cobalt in his shadowed face. She felt him shudder, felt his body coil tight as a spring, felt his arousal jump against her thigh, and she knew he was as hungry for her as she was for him.

It excited her to know he, too, was almost out of control.

He held himself over her, the muscles in his arms and shoulders strained and bulging. She ran her hands over his biceps, down his chest to his taut, rippling belly, then lower, to guide him.

He gasped through clenched teeth when she touched him.

"Careful, *chère*," he muttered hoarsely. "I'm just about over the edge."

As he sank himself into her a low moan escaped her throat. It had been so long. Ever since he'd kissed her on the deck her body had been wound taut as a bowstring. Her emotions had been crying out for release, for relief. She'd tried to deny it, but there was no doubt now. The need inside her had turned to a desperate craving.

Lightning flashed and as it did she tumbled over the edge into blinding passion. She gave herself up to the sensations Cody coaxed from her body.

As the world stopped whirling, Cody's body shuddered and he clutched her against him as he reached his own peak. Dana held him close, moving with him, taking all the pent-up passion he spilled into her. She wanted to cry as he buried his face in the hollow of her neck, his breath hot and ragged.

After a long time, he lifted his head, his blue eyes dilated and questioning. "*Chère?* You okay?" he asked, touching her lower lip with his thumb.

"I'm okay," she whispered, smiling gently at him. And as he lowered his head to kiss her sweetly, she realized she really was.

She didn't know how she'd be in an hour, or in the morning, when she'd had a chance to analyze what she'd done in the cold light of day.

She didn't have a clue how she was going to deal with getting over him again.

But right now, she successfully pushed those thoughts aside and let herself bask in the present. "Live for the moment."

She hadn't realized she'd said it aloud until Cody lifted his head again. "What did you say?"

"Nothing," she said, pulling his head back down to hers. "Nothing at all."

Chapter Eleven

Dana woke up in the middle of the night, hot and thirsty. Cody was asleep next to her, his face shadowed and peaceful in the waning light of the fire. In sleep, with his incredible eyes closed, he looked like an angelic child.

His slim, straight nose, his wide mouth with the generous lips, the ridge of his brow, all the parts of him that, coupled with his intense blue eyes could intimidate the hell out of her, were classic and beautiful when he was relaxed in sleep.

She reached out to touch his lips, but she was afraid she'd wake him, so she clenched her fist and carefully extricated herself from the tangle of quilt and Cody's long legs and pulled the T-shirt on over her head.

In the kitchen she drank a big glass of water, then pushed her sweat-dampened hair out of her face. The storm had passed, and now the air inside the cabin was too warm from the fireplace.

She quietly opened the door and stepped out on the deck, breathing deeply in the rain-washed night. She wrapped her arms around herself and stared out across the lake. Her skin still tingled where Cody's lips had strayed. Her body still thrummed with the aftereffects of his lovemaking. Her brain was still hazy with passion.

She sighed. Tomorrow she would have to go back to the real world. Tomorrow there would still be a madman out there who wanted to kill Cody, and tomorrow he was going to leave her to go track the madman down.

Tomorrow, this night of passion would be another memory that she could stack on top of all the others and try to store away behind the protective wall in her heart.

Dana didn't want to think about tomorrow. She wanted to go back inside and curl up in Cody's arms and pretend they'd just gotten married. She wanted to be pregnant. She wanted to hear Cody say he'd take a desk job out in Metairie or Slidell or Abita Springs so they could finally have their normal boring life.

She wiped her hand across the deck rail, brushing the cool raindrops off the rail to shower down onto the deck floor. Then she brought her wet hand up to her face, relishing its coolness against her hot skin.

"Damn it," she whispered. "Why can't it be easy?" Why couldn't they both want the same thing? Why couldn't she accept the uncertainties of a cop's life? Why couldn't he at least try to stay out of harm's way?

Why ask why, she thought wryly. It does no good.

The door opened and Cody stepped out onto the deck. He came up behind her and wrapped his arms around her and laid his chin against her hair.

"What are you doing out here?" he whispered softly. "I'm supposed to be protecting you and you're standing out here like you don't have a care in the world."

She leaned back against him, savoring the warmth, the safety, of his embrace. "I don't, tonight."

"That's my girl," he muttered dryly. "I try to get you to loosen up for years and you decide to be spontaneous when there's a killer on the loose."

"Thank you for reminding me," she retorted, turning around in his arms and leaning back to look up at him, grinning. "Now who's the party pooper?"

He shrugged. "Just trying to keep you out of trouble, *chère*. You've gotten way too impulsive." He brushed her hair back behind her ears and kissed her tenderly. "Come back inside, and let's act on our impulses one more time."

Dana shivered at the blatantly sexual tone of his voice and the hunger evident in his expression. He lifted her up, and she wrapped her legs around his waist. He kissed her soundly, then kicked open the door and carried her through the living room to the bedroom and tossed her onto the bed and pounced on top of her, laughing.

He pulled her into his arms, kissing her tenderly, slowly, unlike before. Then they had both been desperate, needy, their passion almost savage in its intensity.

Now he was going to take his time. It had been a long time since he'd held her, a long time, and he wanted to savor every inch of her body.

He ran his hand up her slender legs, marveling at the feel of her. Silk and steel. It was the way he always thought of her. He smiled to himself. Just a few hours ago, that steel core had been molten, liquid, burning him when he sank himself into her.

His body reacted to his thoughts, and her eyes widened as she became aware of his blatant arousal. She touched his hand as he caressed her breast, and he lowered his head to take the erect tip in his mouth. Dana gasped and tightened her fingers in his hair as his lips and tongue played over her nipple.

He took his time, coaxing her, teasing her, building the passion slowly this time. He tortured himself by waiting. He held himself back, while he brought her to the brink again and again, until she was whimpering for release. Then he eased himself into her, holding his breath to try to remain in control.

Her eyes burned with emerald fire as he slowly stroked her, waiting, waiting for that moment when he could slip past her defenses and she would give herself over to his love.

After a long, torturous moment, she gasped and arched her back, and Cody laughed softly, triumphant and so turned on he could hardly breathe.

As he watched, her nostrils flared and her breath quickened, and he saw her careful control drain away in the passion of their lovemaking.

Then it happened, and all he could do was experience the lightning flash of sheer ecstasy that encompassed them both.

"CARELESS, MR. MAXWELL," Fontenot whispered as he watched the silhouettes moving together in the darkness from his vantage point near the unmarked police car. "Very careless. And you thought you could beat me."

He smiled to himself. He couldn't have asked for a better situation. The two young lovers rediscovering their love. It fit in perfectly with his plans. He'd known he was right. Four years had made no difference in the way Maxwell felt about his wife.

He wanted to laugh out loud. He wanted to shout his pleasure at the top of his lungs, but he knew better. Unlike Maxwell, he could restrain himself.

Carefully, quietly, he picked the lock on the unmarked police car, and retrieved Mrs. Maxwell's day planner from the back seat where she'd carelessly left it.

He turned to today's entry. Nothing. He flipped a page over to Friday's entry. Ah, perfect.

Friday: buy junk food, buy two romance novels, spend weekend alone at the lake house, reading and eating.

"You will wish you had, Mrs. Maxwell. You will wish you had." He tore the page out of the planner and placed the planner back in precisely the same position it had been in. Then he closed and locked the car door.

Inside the darkened house, the lovers lay still and quiet. *Well, enjoy what pleasure you may find, children. For soon, your pain will be unbearable.*

DANA STEPPED INTO the shower, wishing there was some way she could encapsulate the night before, put it away in a book like a pressed rose. Then the memories would be preserved, and she could be the same person she was before last night. She wouldn't have to learn to live without Cody all over again.

She stood underneath the hot water, hoping it would wash away the treacherous memories of the night, the incredible tenderness with which Cody coaxed her into response, the unbearable pleasure that his hands and mouth and body had given her, the explosive completion he'd shared with her.

Her knees felt water soluble, melting away under

the steamy spray. Dana put out a hand against the wall of the shower to steady herself as the echoes of passion pummeled her more effectively than the shower spray.

She put her head under the pounding water. What kind of idiot was she? She should have known better than to succumb to Cody's carefree charm. She should have remembered why they were here, why *he* was here.

It was all because of his job, the job that consumed him every waking hour. The job of superhero—save the world by day, fall into bed with the little woman at night.

Cutting off the water, Dana tossed her head and reached for a towel.

Superheroes didn't have a lot of time for family. Cody certainly hadn't.

Dana knew he'd loved her. She loved him too. It was obvious last night that none of that had changed. She'd felt as if she was coming home. She'd felt whole for the first time in a long time, when Cody sunk himself into her.

Sure, he loved her.

The trouble was, he didn't love her enough.

Scrubbing her hair dry with the towel, Dana scrubbed away thoughts of how good it had felt to make love with her husband again. *Ex-husband.*

She pulled on shorts and a T-shirt and ran a comb through her wet hair. In the mirror, she saw a woman who'd been well loved. She narrowed her eyes and scrutinized her reflection.

What made the difference? Her eyes sparkled, but that could just be from getting a good night's sleep. Her lips looked softer, redder. Her expression looked—that was it, Dana thought in a mixture of disgust and embarrassment and amusement. She looked serene, satisfied. Kind of a "cat that ate the canary" expression.

She pressed her lips together, splashed water on her burning cheeks and looked again, trying for her lawyer demeanor. She shrugged. Not too bad, if she could just wipe the sparkle out of her eyes.

Now she had to face him, the man she'd spent four years getting over, the man who had destroyed all her careful control in one night of love. The man who would go back to his crazy, dangerous job and leave her to battle with her heart for another four years, or fourteen, or forty.

Stupid! Stupid! Stupid! She felt like banging a legal pad against her forehead. Well, there wasn't going to be a repeat of last night.

Ever. Never ever. She'd revealed way too much of herself. Physically, emotionally, mentally. She'd just have to put some major damage control into effect, starting now.

She took a long breath and opened the bathroom door and almost ran into Cody, who'd obviously been just about to knock. He had a mug of coffee and he proffered it, grinning devilishly.

"Morning," he said, and leaned down to kiss her.

Dana neatly sidestepped him as she took the mug from his fingers. "Aren't you leaving today?" she asked shortly, walking away from him toward the living room.

"I'm fine. Thanks for asking," he said wryly, following her.

She ignored him.

"Ah, *chère,*" he said, coming up behind her. "I need to get back to New Orleans. My buddies are out there looking for Fontenot and I'm sitting up here doing nothing.''

His words cut into Dana's heart. *Doing nothing.* Is that what he thought of what they'd spent practically the entire night doing—nothing? She tried to reerect the barriers around her heart. It wasn't as difficult as she'd been afraid it would be. Not with him talking like that.

It would be even easier if he'd put on some clothes.

''Do you have to walk around in those boxer shorts?'' she groused. ''They're not decent.''

''They cover up more than a bathing suit.''

''That's not the point,'' she retorted. ''The point is the boxers are underwear and are not acceptable attire. The bathing suit has gained an acceptability.''

''Ouch,'' Cody said conversationally. ''I think I just got attacked by the counselor.''

He walked over to her, pinning her in between the bed and the wall, blocking her exit. He put his hand around the back of her neck and caressed her nape, an act that never failed to make her crazy with the need to kiss him.

She closed her eyes and reached for control. ''Cody, stop fooling around. If you're going back to town, you'd better get started.''

''No can do,'' he said, shaking his head slowly, as his lips inched slowly closer to hers.

She pulled her head back and met the resistance of his strong fingers on her neck.

''We have to wait for reinforcements. In fact, it will probably be a couple of hours.''

''Cody, stop it,'' she said in a strained voice.

After a sharp look, Cody backed off. ''What's the

matter, *chère?* Didn't get a good night's sleep?'' His own voice was beginning to sound a bit strained.

"Uh, Cody, I think we should talk about last night.'' Dana walked past him into the kitchen and sat at the table. She felt better sitting down. And it helped to have the battered wooden table as a shield.

Cody came in behind her and got his cup. He leaned back against the sink and watched her, his blue eyes narrowed with suspicion and wariness.

Dana took a deep breath, clutching her mug in both hands and looking at it instead of him. It didn't work very well. Her peripheral vision was filled with the long expanse of her husband's bare flesh—her ex-husband's.

Cody had no modesty. He'd always paraded around with few if any clothes on, and Dana had always loved to watch him. He had a graceful efficiency of movement that reminded her of a big cat, like a cheetah, or a leopard.

With a shake of her head, she pulled her mind away from Cody's body and focused on what she needed to say. "I know this has been an unusual situation for us, being forced together like this because of circumstances beyond our control. And I know that it's only natural that two people who once were intimate might have some dregs of familiarity that would—''

"Dregs?'' Cody stood up straight. "Dregs! What the hell are you talking about. Dana? Could you just spit it out please? You're not making closing remarks here.''

He looked at her oddly and when Dana caught his gaze, she had to look away.

"Or are you?''

"Cody. I think last night was an unfortunate aberration, a natural response between two people who were once married and who are forced to spend time in a place that holds so many..."

"Memories," he finished for her. "I see, counselor. An aberration. So what you're saying is, take a couple of aspirin and if the aberration hits again you might want to consult a doctor? You know, somehow that wasn't the way I saw it."

He glared at her. "I was under the impression we *both* discovered a few things yesterday and last night. It seemed to me like a good starting point. I thought we might try—"

"No!" Dana banged her cup down on the table, desperate to stop him before he could say it.

She couldn't stand to hear what he thought they might try. She didn't want to be faced with the possibility that they could get back together. That was way too scary.

"I mean no, Cody. I don't think it would be a good idea."

"Just what is the problem here, Dana? Why are you acting like I'm the silver-tongued devil and you're about to lose your soul?"

Dana couldn't look at him. If she did, he'd see the shock and the fear in her eyes. She couldn't have described the way she felt any closer than he'd just done in his offhand way.

About to lose her soul. It was a very good description of how she felt—how she had felt last night as the waves of pleasure, and if she were honest, of love, had washed over her as Cody made love to her.

It was the strangest conundrum. She only felt whole with Cody, but she also felt fragmented, like she was

losing her mind and her soul when she let down the
barriers and allowed him in.

"Don't be ridiculous," she snapped in answer to
his question. "You're trying to reduce our situation to
a song lyric or a throwaway line. We are divorced,
Cody. *Divorced.* Doesn't that mean anything to you?"

For an instant, a stark pain shone on Cody's face,
and the pain echoed hollowly in Dana's heart.

"I know we're divorced. You don't have to remind
me of that. I was there, remember?"

"Well, kind of there," she said sarcastically, hating
herself for pushing but unable to stop. She was hurting, aching, for what had been, and what could never
be. And she always had to be the bad guy in these
situations.

She had the feeling Cody would have stayed mar-
ried forever if she hadn't forced the divorce on him.
She spoke to avoid having to deal with that thought.
"You had very little if anything to say. No response.
No argument. It obviously didn't matter to you what
I did."

Cody glared down at her, his eyes sparking with
blue flame. "No, it didn't matter to me. *Much.* What
the hell was I supposed to do? I get out of the hospital,
come home to my loving wife to find out you're sleeping on the couch and our bedroom is set up like a
sickroom, to take care of the recovering invalid."

He poured more coffee, his usually graceful movements jerky and clumsy. He spoke over his shoulder.
"Do you have any idea what it was like? I know you
were hurting, Dana. You'd lost our baby. It had to be
eating you up inside." His shoulders slumped for an
instant, then he straightened and turned around.

"But you acted like some remote sister from the

Catholic hospital, solicitous but distracted, like a goddamn saint who does good works but can't be bothered with actual human reactions. You wouldn't even
touch me, you hardly looked at me.''

He shook his head. ''Then when I was able to go
back to work, you were out of there so fast if my head
wasn't already spinning enough, you finished the job.
Then wham, I got divorce papers in the mail and a
lawyer telling me any further communications should
go through him.

''Matter to me?'' Cody laughed, shortly and deri-
sively. ''It was just the end of my entire life. Why the
hell should it have mattered to me?''

Dana's eyes were burning. Her chest felt as if an
elephant was sitting on it. ''I didn't want to talk about
this now.''

Ever.

She swallowed. ''But maybe it's time. If we get all
the—''

Hurt…

''—if we get everything out in the open, then maybe
we can both move on.''

''Move on…'' Cody's voice was tight and flat.

''Well, sure. I mean, there are obviously unresolved
issues between us. Maybe it's time for some closure.''

''Closure.''

''Would you quit repeating everything I say?''

Cody stared at her. ''I'm just trying to understand,''
he grated.

''I don't see what's so hard for you to understand.
It was all your fault,'' she said desperately, hating the
look on his face, not wanting to face up to the pain
that shone in his blue eyes. She gestured distractedly.

"You had to keep going out there. Every night I sat up wondering if you would make it home."

"I made it home. Every night. I had a job to do. And I did it well. But hey, go ahead, blame me. You've always blamed me for everything."

"That's not fair."

"Well, neither is holding me responsible for everything bad that's ever happened to you." He looked at her, his eyes smoky and dark. "I don't blame you."

She stared at him, shocked by his words. "Blame me? For what? What did I ever do to you?"

"What did you...are you kidding? You *left* me."

CODY'S WORDS ECHOED in Dana's ears. Harsh words, stated bluntly, flatly. As she stared at him, he dropped his gaze, looking down at his hands. Her gaze followed his and she saw the whitened knuckles, the strained tendons in his wrists and the hard, smooth muscles of his forearms. She winced involuntarily, afraid the cup he was holding would shatter in his grip.

You left me.

She remembered what he'd said the other day, in her apartment, too.

I came home to find out my wife was divorcing me and the baby we'd wanted so badly was never going to be born. So don't talk to me about pain. Pain is something I know all about.

Dana's chest was suddenly so tight it felt paralyzed. She gasped for breath. She had been so caught up in what he had done to her by getting shot and almost dying and scaring her half to death, that she had never stopped to consider what she had done to him.

He was right. They'd never really talked after he'd come home from the hospital. She hadn't allowed it.

She'd closed herself off from him, from feeling, from pain.

She had been so caught up in assigning blame that she hadn't considered how she had hurt him. All she'd been able to feel was her own hurt, her own emptiness, her own pain.

"Oh, Cody." She pressed her hands against her chest, trying to ease the heavy weight that made it so hard to breathe, as her throat clogged. "I am so, so sorry."

She looked up at him, surprised at how hazy and watery he looked. She blinked and a stray tear slid down her cheek. "I was scared. I hadn't been feeling well for a couple of days. I knew something was wrong with the baby." She spread her fingers over her flat belly as she talked. "You were…gone, on some undercover operation. I hadn't heard from you, hadn't seen you, for days. I w-waited there in that apartment, and it was just like all the times…all the times Mama and I sat up waiting for Daddy to come home." She clenched her fists on the table and looked down at them, seeing instead the anxious, terrified look in her mother's eyes.

"We'd wait and wait, sometimes for weeks, and maybe he'd call, or send an envelope with some money. But then the calls would stop, and Mama would ask me to come sleep in the bed with her. Only we wouldn't sleep. We'd just lie there, waiting. She'd look at me with that awful terror in her eyes, and I'd pat her h-hand—"

She stopped. Her voice had cracked. She curled her fingers against the scarred wood of the table. "I'd pat her hand and tell her I was sure he'd be back soon."

"*Chère*—"

She shook her head. "I was so sure he'd be back. Every single time. I was sure. Because he was my daddy, and he promised me." She blinked, and two fat tears escaped and rolled down her cheeks.

"And every time, eventually, he came home. But then, my twelfth birthday came, and he'd promised me he'd be there...you know? But he wasn't. The weeks turned into months, and we didn't hear from him. My thirteenth birthday came and went, and sometime during that year my mother's eyes turned from scared to sad."

She shrugged and glanced up at Cody, biting her lip to keep it from quivering. She could hear the thickness of tears in her voice. "Then one day the police called. They'd found a car when they drained a lake. He'd lost control on a rickety country bridge. Drowned. His driver's license was laminated." She shuddered violently, then covered her mouth with her hands.

Chapter Twelve

Cody had watched Dana with a dawning horror, as she relived something he couldn't even begin to understand. He longed to wrap his arms around her trembling shoulders, but he didn't. The thread she was hanging on to was so fragile right now. She was so breakable.

Her pale face, her trembling hands that barely held the hysteria at bay, her stiff, thin shoulders, all those things were more precious to him than ever. He stood, helpless, as a new, terrible understanding dawned in him.

Waiting. That was what scared her so. The waiting. Sitting, being brave, wondering if this would be the time he didn't come home, just like her father. Now he knew what kept her from letting go. Fear. Fear, and a sadness he could never imagine.

If it were the last thing he ever did, he would banish that fear from her eyes.

After a few moments, she put her hands, palm down, on the table again. "There's a place inside me, Cody," she said in a small voice. "A place that I have to keep closed off. Because the...the pain in there is so bad…'' She gestured helplessly and smiled a sad little smile. ''I don't think I could stand it.''

With every fiber of his being, he wanted to reach out and pull her close, but he knew her well enough to know that she didn't want to be held right now. Especially by him.

So, forcing a lightness he was far from feeling into his voice, he spoke quietly. ''I'm right here, *chère*. I can help you. You can count on me.''

She looked up, and he saw in her face that his attempt at lightness hadn't worked. She was poised, halfway between the past and the present, and nothing he could say right now would convince her that he was any more dependable than her father.

''Dana, please. I want to help.''

He watched as she drew strength from somewhere and straightened up. She closed her eyes tight, then opened them again, and her look was accusatory. ''While you were in surgery, I lost my baby. Alone, in a public bathroom in the surgical intensive care waiting room. It was too much. I can't go through it again, Cody. There's no room in me for any more hurt.''

Cody's heart was filled to bursting, and a suspicious stinging was starting behind his eyes. ''Come here.'' He reached out to her, and she almost yielded, but then she pulled back.

She held up a hand, palm out. ''Don't, Cody. Please don't ever touch me again.''

Cody froze at her words. He saw the tears in her eyes, and he knew she loved him.

But she would rather live without love than take the chance of being hurt, of losing him like she lost her father. He understood her fear. *But, oh God, it hurt.*

Cody wanted to kill the bastard who hadn't cared enough about his family to stay with them, to give of himself to keep them safe.

She stood and put her cup in the sink, then turned back toward him. "Please don't try to see me again, Cody. I'd appreciate it."

She whirled and stalked off to the bedroom, her slender back stiff, her chin held high.

He loved her so much. There was no question about that. He'd loved Dana from the first minute he'd set eyes on her.

The very things he loved were the things that kept her from him now. Her strength. Her determination. Her courage. Now he knew even better just how strong and courageous she really was.

But did she have to be so stubborn?

He shouldn't have said what he did to her, but it was the truth. Mostly. He really didn't blame her. He hadn't blamed her for leaving him. But sometimes, deep in the night when the air was too muggy to sleep and the loneliness crept in to suffocate him, he blamed her for not loving him enough to put up with him.

He blamed her for wanting her safe, orderly life more than she wanted him.

He was a cop. It was in his blood. There was nothing he could do about that. His grandfather had come to New Orleans from Ireland to start over, and had walked a beat for thirty years.

There was nothing as exciting as pitting yourself against a worthy adversary. Nothing as satisfying as putting a murderer away. Nothing.

Cody stopped his thoughts right there. He was lying to himself. Last night had made him start thinking about things, made him look back at his life and wonder if he'd made the right choices. And Dana's words this morning only reinforced the doubt that was beginning to grow.

He'd missed a lot.

What if watching his own child being born was more exciting than anything he'd ever done?

What if holding his own child in his arms surpassed the satisfaction of capturing a murderer?

What if a quiet, safe life with the woman he loved was better than being a hotshot detective?

What if living quietly, surrounded by love, was better than dying heroically?

He looked toward the bedroom, wanting to rush in there and tell Dana about all his newfound insights, but she was upset and scared. And damned if he wasn't going to have to upset and scare her even more, before he could even think about making up to her for all the ways he'd failed her in the past.

It didn't matter what great insights he'd had. It didn't matter that she'd finally opened up to him and told him things she'd never told anyone.

Later, they needed to talk. Right now, there were other, more important considerations than Dana's feelings. There was her life. He glanced at his watch.

He needed to take a look around, to be sure Fontenot hadn't tracked them here. And he needed to check in with the captain to see what the situation was.

Grabbing his cell phone, he walked outside. He looked around. Everything still seemed quiet and deserted. The lake was placid, the air still. He stopped and listened. Nothing.

The hairs on the back of his neck prickled, and he turned around, staring back up toward the house. What was wrong, then? There was nothing out of the ordinary that he could see, or hear. It almost seemed too quiet.

Frowning, he punched in the numbers for the precinct, stopping when he heard a familiar roar. As his best friend and partner's battered Chevy roared up, Cody stuck the cell phone back in its holder on his belt and stood up.

What the hell was Dev doing here? A mixture of relief and apprehension settled hard on his chest.

"Dev! Where y'at?" he called, walking toward his buddy's ancient car, shaking his head at its condition and the mud it had gathered on its trip here.

"Damn it, Cody," Dev grumbled as he surveyed his treasured car. "This gumbo mud's going to eat the paint right off my babe."

Cody grinned. "Come on, Dev. Like there's any paint left on it to eat off. All I see is primer. Why didn't you bring one of the department's four-wheelers?"

Dev turned to Cody. "I wasn't much interested in announcing to the world that I'm a cop."

Cody stiffened. "Why? What's the deal, Dev? You got something on Fontenot?" His pulse sped up and his muscles tensed, but it wasn't the old familiar thrill of the chase. It was fear, fear for Dana.

He glanced up at the house again, and wiped his face. "Well?" he insisted, when Dev hesitated.

"Code, there's something wrong with the picture."

Cody's mouth went dry in sudden apprehension. "I knew it. What is it? It's too pat, isn't it?"

Dev nodded. "The man went to a lot of trouble to rent a car without leaving a trail, but we traced him and the car to Pensacola, and of course we took care of Dana's sister."

The big detective's face lightened and his black eyes sparkled like polished ebony. "And let me tell you that baby sister is something. I mean Dana is a knockout, all right, but Angie is a stunner. What a woman!"

"Dev!"

"Okay, okay. I was beginning to think your buddy Fontenot had lost his touch. I mean tracing him to the rental car agency was not easy, but it was hardly on the same par with his usual tricks."

Cody's stomach clenched. "So you're saying…"

"He covered his tracks, but not too well."

"You think he was baiting us?"

Dev rubbed his neck and grimaced. "You could say that. The car turned up abandoned, just on the other side of Pensacola, with a dead fish in it."

Cody stared at his friend. "A dead fish?"

"Yup." Dev nodded, looking expectantly at his friend. "A dead fish. A red herring."

"I knew it! It was too easy. Damn!" Cody pounded his fist against the hood of the Chevy.

"Hey, watch the car."

"So you lost his trail? And you're sure he did nothing to Dana's sister, or the kids? There was nothing out of place? Nothing unusual?"

"Oh, he did something, all right. He left a page from Dana's day planner on Angie's doorstep."

Cody felt the blood drain from his face. He racked his brain, trying to remember the last time he'd seen her planner. "What day?"

Dev pulled a plastic bag with a sheet of paper inside it from his jacket pocket.

With fingers that he couldn't stop from trembling, Cody took the bag. He knew what he would see before he looked, but he stared in fascination at the pale green page. It was Friday's page, and there, written in her precise handwriting, was Dana's note to herself.

Buy junk food, buy two romance novels, spend weekend alone at the lake house, reading and eating.

Dev caught the bag as it dropped from Cody's hand. "Friday. Two days ago. When did Dana last have it?"

A memory seared Cody's brain. "On the way up here," he said, his jaw clenched tight. "She had some coupons for coffee in it."

Dev stiffened and glanced up at the lake house. "You know where it is now?" he asked, the black intensity in his eyes belying his casual question.

Cody followed his gaze, frowning, then turned and rushed over to the car.

The doors were locked, and inside, on the back seat, where she must have left it when they took the groceries in, was Dana's day planner. It was zipped closed, and the little gold nameplate on the front shone dully in the shadows.

Cody's blood ran cold. "He's been here. That son of a bitch has been here. He's been watching us."

Behind him, Dev swore softly and colorfully. "We need to get somebody up here to go over the car."

"There's no point in that. I know, I know, procedure. But think about it, Dev. He doesn't care if we know he's been here. He wants us to know. It will feed his ego to have the car dusted for prints. He's laughing at us."

He turned around, scanning the thick foliage that surrounded the inlet and the house. He pushed his fingers through his hair and wiped his face. "God, Dev. I've been goofing off up here, playing house with

Dana. I let myself forget just how good the bastard is.''

Dev chuckled. ''You two have been playing house? You patching things up?''

Cody shook his head and rubbed his neck. ''Don't, Dev. She's too upset. And she has a right to be. Damn. How could I have let him get so close? How could I have been such an idiot? He could have killed her.''

''He's after *you*.''

''Hell, yeah, he's after me. And he'll use her if he can. Damn it!'' Cody hit the car with his doubled fists, relishing the pain that shot up his arms. ''What was I thinking? I should have been after him.''

''Whoa, Code. Stay cool.'' Dev lost his cheerful demeanor and straightened to his full six-feet-three-inch frame. His cold black eyes skimmed the horizon. ''Just how removed from you and Dana is this place? How did he trace you here?''

Cody shook his head. ''The house belonged to a friend of Dana's granddad, an old Cajun who liked his privacy, to say the least. It's in the old man's name. It's like I told the captain. There shouldn't have been any way to trace it to Dana.''

''What about the electricity?''

''It has its own generator. I cranked it up when we got here.'' Cody pulled out his revolver and checked it. ''We've got to get Dana out of here.'' He squinted up at the house, which looked peaceful. Deceptively peaceful.

''What about water and sewer? Property taxes?''

''Dana's brother, Greg, arranged for a local to take care of all that a long time ago. Hell!''

''What?'' Dev cocked an eyebrow in his direction.

''I don't know how Greg pays the local guy.''

Dev grimaced. "Check probably. Where does he live?"

"In Iowa, but still…"

"Yeah, still."

Cody tensed. "So how long has it been since anyone has verified Fontenot's whereabouts? He could have been here any time in the past two days. The page wasn't missing when we got here Friday night. She'd have noticed."

"You sure? She was pretty upset."

Cody shot Dev a look.

"Okay. Yeah. This is Dana we're talking about."

A tiny smile curved Cody's mouth. "Yeah. She'd have noticed."

"Well, the last time he was actually spotted was at the rental car agency, yesterday morning. Saturday. And the page showed up on Angie's doorstep this morning." Dev shrugged his shoulders, settling his jacket, and brushed his fingers across the bulge of his own weapon. "There's something else."

"What?"

"Yesterday afternoon, a woman was murdered, her neck snapped. Right on the street near where the rental car was found. And her car is missing. It's a real junker, according to some neighbors. Not what you'd expect Fontenot to drive."

"That's how he got here. He was here last night. Probably watching us, while we were… God! How could I have been so stupid?" Cody wrapped his hand around his gun. "We've got to assume he's here, Dev."

"Let's get you two out of here."

Cody shook his head. "Let's get Dana out of here.

I'm going to get Fontenot. We can't underestimate him.''

''We'll get him, my friend. Now I'm calling for backup.''

Cody shot a grateful look at Devereaux Gautier. ''Thanks, friend.''

DANA THREW CLOTHES into her bag, her brain whirling with the implications of Cody's words, her chest squeezing so tightly it hurt to breathe.

I didn't blame you.

You left me.

Remembering back, Dana was amazed at how callous she must have seemed. In reality, she'd been numb, running on nervous energy and caffeine, desperate to get away from Cody as soon as possible because he was the embodiment of everything she'd lost.

Oh, God, how deeply she had hurt him.

While he'd been in the hospital, he'd lost his family, just as she had. When she should have been there for him, while he was recuperating from brain surgery, where had she been? *In a fog of self-pity and grief, that's where.*

How could she have done that to him? Her chest squeezed tight as she realized the pain she'd put him through.

He'd lost the chance to have a child, too, but he'd gone right on. He'd had to, she realized now.

He'd returned to work as soon as he'd been able, sooner than he should have. He'd agreed to all her terms for the divorce as if he hadn't really cared one way or the other. He'd let her take whatever she'd wanted without protest.

He'd been distracted, remote, removed from it all.

As she thought back, armed with her new realization, she could see that the dullness in his eyes was grief, that the slump in his shoulders was defeat, rather than just a lack of interest in the whole divorce. And the tense whiteness around his mouth and the stiffness in his bearing had been hurt, not just impatience to have it all over and done.

It was too much to take in right now, just how much she must have hurt him, so with a great effort of will she stopped the thoughts and concentrated on being angry with him for going back to New Orleans. That was easier to deal with.

She muttered to herself as she tossed her sandals into the bag. "If you think you're going off to New Orleans and leaving me here with some local hick cop who can't even find his bullet, you're crazy, Cody." She leaned over the bed to retrieve her hairbrush.

Suddenly, she heard a sound behind her. A soft sound, like a swish of cloth. She started to turn. "Cody?"

Something smelly and hot covered her head.

She couldn't breathe. She couldn't see. Her legs were kicked out from under her and she was dragged across the floor.

She tried to scream, but when she took a deep breath, all she got was a lungful of dust and lint.

She coughed, choked, coughed again.

Then, like a flash of lightning, she knew. It was Fontenot. Adrenaline shot through her, and she forced air into her burning lungs and screamed.

Fontenot whacked her upside the head with something heavy. Pain exploded in her brain. Only the meager cushion of the blanket kept her from being knocked unconscious.

Dazed and nauseated, and choking from the dust, she kicked feebly at the hands that tugged her feet with surprisingly efficient strength. He pulled her out the back door. She heard its familiar creak and yelped when her head bumped on the threshold.

She rolled and kicked, trying to get her feet under her, screaming at the top of her lungs for Cody.

"Screaming won't help, Mrs. Maxwell." The voice was muffled, but she understood the words. "He can't hear you."

Fontenot kicked her, then hit her in the head again. "I do wish you would stop struggling. It would make things so much easier."

She recognized his voice, and it made her skin crawl. It was a strange voice, low and hoarse, soft but grating. Its very quietness belied the sheer insanity of his words.

"Stop! Why are you doing this?" Dana kept yelling, futile as it was.

She was turned roughly, and some kind of heavy strapping or tape was wrapped around her midsection, pinning her arms to her sides and tangling the blanket even more efficiently around her.

The restraints cut off what little air she'd had to breathe. She gasped blindly, desperate to fill her lungs with untainted air. If she didn't get a full breath soon, she would die.

"This will just take a moment, Mrs. Maxwell. You'll forgive me if I'm in a bit of a hurry. I usually am much neater."

He easily got her legs trussed despite her desperate kicking, and Dana was overwhelmed by something she'd never experienced in her life. Terrifying, nauseating claustrophobia. She couldn't see. She couldn't breathe. She couldn't move.

She thrashed. Gasped and coughed, straining for air.

Panic stole the last dregs of coherence and nothing at all made any sense. She whimpered hoarsely and struggled weakly, fast running out of energy and will.

A ripping sound—a flash of metal—blinding sunlight and blessed, blessed air.

She gulped and coughed, then sucked air in through her mouth, preparing to scream.

Chapter Thirteen

Fontenot jerked Dana upright and ripped the cut in the blanket wider, until he could push it down on her shoulders, exposing her face. Then he slapped her with his open palm.

"You really must be quiet. Here's a little something to help." He plastered a strip of tape across her mouth, cutting off any sound she might have made.

She squinted against the bright sunlight. Fontenot's shadow loomed over her head. Her first glimpse of her captor had confirmed that it was him. His pale hair, thinning on top, his puffy eyes, shining madly. Those wet, pink lips, smiling blandly at her, as if he were making party conversation.

"Now, if you don't mind, it would be a very good idea if we moved away from the house. Quickly."

"Why? What have you done?" Her words were nothing but desperate grunts, muffled by the tape, as he pushed her toward the woods.

She fell, encumbered by the bindings around her thighs just above her knees.

Cursing under his breath, he picked her up again, holding on to her. "Really, Mrs. Maxwell. Please try.

Otherwise I might have to really kill you. Now, come on. We've got a show to attend.''

Fontenot was mad. Cody was right. A streak of panic sheared her breath as Cody's words slammed into her mind.

There's a madman out there who wants to kill me, and he won't mind killing you to get to me.

"Let me go, you son of a bitch." She tried to scream the words, but Fontenot had done a good job of gagging her. She couldn't get enough breath to yell and she couldn't move her mouth.

He grabbed the end of the strap he'd wrapped around her and pulled her along behind him as he climbed up into the wooded area above the backwater. Dana had no choice but to follow as best she could. With her knees bound she could do little more than shuffle. If she fell again, he would just drag her, or kill her.

They were behind the house, up above the swampy little inlet. They ought to be visible from the pier.

Where was Cody? Why wasn't he rescuing her? Hadn't he heard her scream?

Had Fontenot done something to him?

Oh, God, no! Don't let Cody be dead. He'd gone out to look around. Maybe Fontenot hadn't seen him. Maybe Cody was okay. If he was, he'd rescue her.

Fontenot finally stopped and Dana tried to catch her breath. She worked her mouth but the tape was stuck fast. She tried to wipe it off against her shoulder, but the stupid edge of the blanket just flopped back and forth. Desperately she looked around her for something, anything she could use to escape.

"Here we are," Fontenot said, smiling at her serenely. "Best seats in the house." He turned her around and pushed her down on the ground.

He smiled and hummed to himself as he settled beside her, picking invisible lint off his impeccably tailored suit. Dana watched him in horror. He was insane. A maniac, just like Cody said. Panic escalated into unrelenting terror inside her.

"What have you done with Cody?" she asked, although her words sounded like moans behind the tape.

Fontenot put his arm around her shoulders and pulled her close. He smelled like cologne, a familiar scent that lent an eerie air of normalcy to the insane situation she found herself in. His hand, wrapped around her exposed shoulder, was clammy and soft. Too soft. She shuddered at his touch.

"Now, now, sweetheart, calm down," his oily voice whispered in her ear. "Didn't I promise you a show? Well, the curtain is about to go up on my greatest achievement. If I could dim the lights, I would, but I'm not in charge of stage direction, so I'll just have to make do with what the Lord has provided."

Dana swallowed against nauseating fear and disgust. He was certifiable.

"Look, Mrs. Maxwell," Fontenot said, a note of barely suppressed excitement in his voice. "Watch carefully now. The show is about to begin. Pardon me for pointing."

Dana looked in the direction he indicated. From their vantage point above the inlet, they had a clear view of the stretch of land and swamp and water in front of the lake house. She spotted Dev's battered Chevy, and a few feet away, headed for the pier, she saw Dev and Cody.

What was Dev doing here? Was Dev the one Cody

had sent for to watch her? A surge of hope washed through her. Dev and Cody were a dauntless team. Alone, Cody could do just about anything. But together, the two of them were truly invincible.

She relaxed a bit. She didn't know how they would rescue her, but she had confidence in her husband and his partner. If anyone could get Fontenot, they could.

She saw them talking, Cody gesticulating in that way he had and Dev laying his hand on Cody's arm, trying to reassure him, Dana was sure. They were arguing about something.

Conscious of the maniac beside her, Dana found it hard to concentrate on what she was seeing before her. She considered vaulting up, making a scene, but a quick look around told her Fontenot had chosen his vantage point well.

Once again Cody was right. Fontenot was a genius. He could not have chosen a better place from which to view the area below the lake house. It would be impossible for Dana to attract the attention of the two men, up here, surrounded by trees and underbrush as they were. Besides, Fontenot's arm was around her shoulders and Dana was certain he would do whatever he deemed necessary to keep her from alerting Cody.

So she waited and watched Cody and Dev come to some sort of conclusion, a hundred yards away from her, and as good as halfway around the world.

They turned and walked toward the unmarked car. Cody leaned over and looked inside, then hit the car in obvious fury and frustration. Dev said something to him, and Cody drew his service revolver.

The man beside her chuckled, a supremely fiendish sound. "Ah. So finally, Detective Maxwell is beginning to understand."

Understand what? Dana wanted to scream. She was caught up in a terror more profound than anything she had ever felt before. It tightened the skin of her scalp. It nauseated her. She knew, beyond a shadow of a doubt, that she was about to see something too horrible to put into words.

"Don't, please," she begged the maniac whose arm encircled her so gently, whose ominously pleasant voice still hummed in her ear.

She couldn't speak around the tape that covered her mouth, but she still tried. "Please don't hurt him," she begged.

As if he knew what she'd said, Fontenot patted her shoulder. "Don't you worry about a thing, Mrs. Maxwell. I can assure you this will be an unforgettable experience. You'll remember it for the rest of your life." He laughed. "The rest of your life. That's a good one."

CODY LISTENED TO DEV talking to Captain Hamilton on his cell phone. "You tell him I'm perfectly healthy."

Dev nodded.

Cody gestured with his gun. "I'm going up to the house. I don't like the idea of Dana being up there by herself. How soon can they get us some backup up here?"

Dev closed his phone. "They're sending the local guys right now, and Hamilton's got three units from Metairie responding."

"Good." Cody nodded. "Let's get up to—"

A deafening roar drowned out all other sound. Light flashed. Blinding light.

Cody whirled toward the sound.

His heart stopped.

White-hot light erupted out of the top of the lake house as the deafening thunder roiled all around them.

Then the world exploded around Cody in slow motion. Pieces of wood, fragments of metal, floated in the air, some bright with fire, others just dark specks against the sky.

To Cody, it seemed to go on and on and on, rising upward, billowing out, black smoke following the blinding light, the deafening roar of the explosion followed by the dull sound of fire as it sucked oxygen from the air.

"No-o-o-o!" Someone shouted, the word torn agonizingly from his throat. "Oh, God, no!"

Cody forced his numbed legs to move.

"No!" the voice screamed again. "Dana! God, please!"

And Cody realized it was him, realized his throat burned, his arms and legs felt wooden, his soul had died.

He ran clumsily, blindly toward the exploding building, his breath ragged gasps, his heart slamming against his chest as if desperate to break free, his legs like wooden sticks that didn't work.

Vaguely, distractedly, he noticed the heat. It billowed around him like a live thing. It rose up before him like an invisible wall, holding him back.

"Dana!"

He had to get her out. She'd burn up in there. He ran toward the house, toward the deck that was no longer there.

A burning plank slammed into his shoulder, but he dodged it and kept going. Dana was in the bedroom, wasn't she?

It looked as though the bedroom hadn't been blown completely apart. He had to get her out. *Hurry!*

He climbed toward that side of the house, stumbling, falling, getting up again. A rush of fire engulfed the wood.

"Dana! Get out!" he screamed desperately, hopelessly, pushing burning planks aside, scrambling toward the bedroom, falling over and over. His feet slipped on the wet grass of the hill, and he scrambled, fighting against the slick dew, to get up again.

"Dana!" he screamed. *Please!*

He couldn't see. He rubbed frantically at his eyes and kept climbing toward the raging inferno that had been the lake house, toward Dana. He had to get to her. He had to.

The fire was getting too hot. She'd burn up in there. Suddenly, something tackled him from behind and dragged him backward. Cody whirled and gained his feet, then threw a punch at Dev, who deftly side-stepped it.

"Cody! Stop!" Dev shouted, grabbing at Cody's flailing arms.

"Dana!" Cody yelled. "Got to get her out! Get the hell out of my way!" He threw another punch but lost his balance and fell into the bigger man's arms.

He pushed against Dev's chest as hard as he could. "What are you doing? Get out of my way!" Dev was trying to stop him from getting to Dana.

Dev locked him in a bear hug. "Stop! It's too late. God, Code, it's too late!"

Cody heard Dev's words, but he couldn't—he wouldn't accept them.

"No! Dev! Let me go, goddamn you. Let me go!" He struggled with the strength of desperation, of panic, of awful horror too great to imagine. The horror of Dana trapped up there, in that burning house.

He wrenched out of his partner's grasp and lunged back toward the burning pile of rubble that had once been a house.

"Oh, God. Oh, God, Dana!" he rasped, because he could no longer scream. He grabbed another piece of burning wood just as Dev tackled him again.

Cody whirled and hit Dev on the side of the head with the piece of wood, then his own head exploded into light, and then into darkness.

ABOVE THEM, HIDDEN by foliage and underbrush, Dana felt her heart die in her breast as she watched Cody's futile struggle.

"No, oh no, oh no!" Dana moaned behind the tape as Dev dragged Cody, unconscious, back down the hill. Her heart hurt so badly she thought she would die.

She'd watched the whole thing. She hadn't even been able to blink as the horrific scene had played out before her. She hadn't taken her eyes off Cody as the lake house exploded into a fireball.

Over the roar of the explosion, she'd heard him scream her name, and the sound had torn through her like a knife through rotten cloth. Even from this distance, she'd seen the stark, white agony in his face.

She'd watched her husband as he realized his wife was dead.

It would have hurt less if Fontenot had ripped her heart out with his bare hands.

Over and over again, Cody had dragged himself up and headed toward the burning wreckage of the lake house. A mixture of helpless gratitude and blinding compassion engulfed her as Dev tackled Cody again and again, saving him from the inferno.

Cody would kill himself to get to her.

Dana didn't think she could hurt any more, but her thoughts dug deep, bloody furrows on her soul as her brain absorbed what she'd seen.

He'd been determined—desperate—to save her. He'd run toward the deadly fire. He'd screamed her name, shouted *No!* to the heavens over and over again. He'd grabbed burning boards with his bare hands. He'd even hit Dev with a smoldering board.

And she knew if Dev hadn't stopped him, if Dev hadn't knocked him out cold, Cody would have thrown himself into the fire because he thought she was there.

If it had been another man whose wife was trapped in a burning building, Cody would have done what Dev had. He'd have acted responsibly to keep the man from killing himself to save someone who was almost certainly already dead.

But Cody hadn't been the competent, responsible cop at that moment. He'd been a man who had lost everything.

Dana's heart broke as she realized something else. She had not only seen a man trying to save a life. She'd watched her husband as he'd lost the most precious thing in his world.

Dana sobbed, her eyes streaming, her nose running. She'd never known he loved her that much. She'd never realized how much he cared.

Her whole body ached with grief, with sadness, for Cody, who thought she was dead. She cried for him and for herself, and with every sob, she cursed the man who had set this unspeakable drama in motion.

Beside her, Fontenot sat spellbound. His breaths were short and rapid, his upper lip beaded with sweat. His eyes were dilated. He licked his lips, chasing droplets of sweat with his tongue.

"Magnificent," he breathed in that quiet, mad voice. "Brilliant. I really should have videotaped it. But then, does true art, true genius, really need an audience?" He rubbed his hands together, and Dana noticed they were trembling.

She tensed, willing herself to run, but the unyielding tape around her knees, her midsection and arms, her shoulders, reminded her she was trussed like a turkey, and helpless. Panic welled within her as Fontenot drew a long, shuddering breath and continued with his deranged muttering.

"Art is art, and genius is undeniable, whether presented to the world or not. Perhaps, even, one could argue that the most exquisite genius is always unappreciated."

Dana watched him in unbearable horror. He was insane, the most insane person she had ever seen.

"Mark my words, Mrs. Maxwell. Some day, some day my name will be known. Some day, they all will have to acknowledge my superiority."

Calmly, Fontenot pulled a handkerchief from his pocket and blotted the sweat from his lip and brow. Then he stood.

"Come, Mrs. Maxwell. This part of our drama is ended now. We need to go."

She turned and looked back down the hill, where Dev crouched over Cody, a cell phone in one hand, the other touching the side of his head where Cody had connected with the burning two-by-four.

Even from this far away, Dana saw how shaken Dev

was. She'd never seen the big detective react to anything. She'd always thought he was impermeable to normal, human frailties like fear, or grief. But what the madman beside her had done had even broken through Dev's defenses.

And Cody. *Oh, Cody.* Dev must have dealt him a crushing blow, because he was unconscious, lying limp on the ground. Dana sent a silent prayer of thanks to Dev Gautier for taking care of her husband.

"Come, Mrs. Maxwell." Fontenot hauled her upright. "Why, you're trembling. I'm humbled and gratified that you were so…affected by the performance." He laughed, a low, demented sound. "Call me a show-off, but I do so enjoy an appreciative audience."

His strength and brutality belied his soft voice as he dragged her bodily through the woods, then pulled her up against a dirty wreck of a car. He grabbed her hair and forced her head back so she had to look at him. One gloved finger touched a tear that was just spilling over from her eye.

"Ah, dear lady. Thank you for this." He held up the teardrop until it caught the sun in a prism of color. Then he touched it to his tongue. "Tears just may be the perfect elixir of emotion. They combine pain, effort, love, humiliation, grief, anger. Ah. Exquisite." He smiled serenely. "Your husband obviously does love you very much. That's good." He nodded. "Yes. That is good. I was so pleased to see that you two…renewed your physical bond last night. That fits in very well with my plans."

Dana stared at him in shock. "You watched?"

He smiled and touched her cheek, rubbing his thumb over the ragged edge of duct tape. "It is so endearing, that you continue to try and talk, even though you can hardly move your lips. It's amusing to listen to your moans and grunts, and try to decipher them.''

He ran his hand down the side of her neck, and Dana shuddered in revulsion. ''I'm positive you exclaimed 'You watched?' in horror. Yes, Mrs. Maxwell. I watched. And in a rather base way, it was entertaining.'' He pulled the blanket back over her head. ''Now we really must be going.'' Opening the car door, he pushed her into the floorboard of the back seat.

''You ghoul,'' she muttered through the tape on her mouth, struggling to breathe inside the musty blanket. But as he started the car, he just hummed.

''You deserve to die the most horrible of deaths. You deserve the worst I can think of, and I swear to God if it's the last thing I do, I'll make you pay for what you've done to Cody.''

''Now, Mrs. Maxwell,'' Fontenot said reasonably. ''You're going to wear yourself out. Just lie still. We'll be there soon, well before dark.'' He continued to talk. Dana could barely hear him.

''Now we'll find out just how quickly the police discover that there are no human remains in the house. I calculate that it will take them most of the evening, which should give me plenty of time to finish my preparations. I only hope it won't take them much longer than that. I do so look forward to my next encounter with your husband. If he were just a more worthy opponent…'' Fontenot sighed. ''You cannot imagine how annoying it is to have to constantly deal with imbeciles.''

Dana lay still, trying to conserve her energy. She knew she was going to need every ounce of strength she possessed in the next several hours. If she lived.

But she wasn't through with him yet. Even though Fontenot wouldn't understand a word she said, she had to finish her promise. "You will die, Fontenot," she swore. "That's a promise. And if I can make you suffer like you've made Cody suffer, I'll be satisfied."

She'd made an oath, and she would keep it until she died.

Chapter Fourteen

Cody came starkly awake. The first thing he noticed was pain, searing pain, in his hands and arms. He opened his eyes, but everything was hazy, watery. He closed them again and tried to ground himself. He was lying down, on a pallet of some sort, and he was damned uncomfortable. As he struggled to regain some semblance of control over his hazy brain, he licked dry lips, and tasted blood and smoke.

All this flitted through his brain in a split second. What had happened to him? He moved, and felt the harsh cut of metal into the skin of his wrists. He was handcuffed.

Jerking his arms, sending spears of pain through them, he looked around. Handcuffed wasn't all. He was restrained, tied to a stretcher, which two men in white were lifting into the back of an ambulance.

Cody struggled against his bonds and bellowed. "Dev, goddamn it! Where are you? What the hell's going on?" His throat burned and his voice came out as no more than a hoarse whisper.

Suddenly, as brutally and instantly as the explosion had rent the air, Cody remembered, and his heart shattered.

No! Oh, God, Dana!

"Dana!" he screamed hoarsely. "Dev!" He struggled some more, and succeeded in ripping the Velcro restraints off one arm.

"Goddamn it, somebody let me up! I've got to find her! Help me!"

A shadow fell over his face and he felt a pinprick in his arm.

"Don't! Don't drug me! I've got to...find...Dana."

The world closed in on him and the pain in his hands and arms lessened. But even as he lost consciousness, Cody realized the drug they'd given him hadn't lessened the pain in his heart at all.

DEVEREAUX GAUTIER DROVE UP to the Lucky Seven Motel just south of Slidell. It was the closest motel to the explosion site. He sat behind the wheel of the car and stared at his soot-covered hands. He'd had the devil of a time explaining the whole story to the local sheriff. After a lengthy discussion, the headache where Cody had smacked him with a smoldering two-by-four was raging out of control.

So he'd lifted the sheriff by his collar and growled right in his face. "My partner's wife was in the house when it went up. I had a little trouble convincing him it wasn't a good idea to rush into the fire to save her. That clear enough for you?"

The sheriff had calmed down and helped them get Cody into the ambulance, but after the paramedics checked him over and bandaged his hands and forearms, they said he needed to be hospitalized.

Dev had to spend another half hour convincing them that as a former medic in the marines he was perfectly qualified and capable of administering morphine by injection if Cody woke up in pain. As lies went, he thought, it was a pretty good one.

Then he'd checked them into a room at the motel, got Cody bedded down with another dose of morphine, borrowed a local deputy to watch him and headed back to the explosion site.

Donning a spare set of firefighter gear, he'd gone through the smoldering wreckage alongside the local police and the firefighters. He'd set his jaw in grim determination, and gone over every inch of the pile of smoking rubble that had once been the lake house. In the bedroom, they found scraps and pieces of clothing. In the kitchen area and scattered all over the site were burned carcasses of crawfish. There was nothing left of the living room and deck.

Every time one of the men shouted, every time Dev saw something unusual, his heart flipped painfully in his chest. But he gritted his teeth and continued searching.

He'd never forgive himself if he let someone else find Dana. It was his responsibility, as Cody's partner, and as his best friend. He couldn't let him down.

Now he was through. They were all through, except the arson investigators. There were still a lot of unanswered questions. There was one conclusion everyone shared, from the arson expert to the sheriff to the fire chief to Dev himself.

There were no human remains found on the scene. None at all.

Dev sat in his car and pushed grimy, soot-stained hands through his hair and rubbed his burning eyes. He didn't know Dana as well as he knew Cody, since they'd been divorced for the past four years. But he knew Cody still loved her.

Cody thought Dana was dead. Dev had been prepared to stay out there all night, if that was what it took, to make sure there was no doubt. There wasn't. The official announcement would come tomorrow. No human remains. It wasn't hard to make the next jump in logic.

No human remains equaled Fontenot had Dana.

Dev shuddered. What was Cody going to do when he found out?

He profoundly hoped his friend and partner would sleep until morning. The New Orleans police, the Slidell police, in fact everyone in the state had been notified that Fontenot was on the loose with a possible hostage. Maybe by morning they'd have some news.

Now Dev had to go in and face Cody. He didn't know what he dreaded more—telling Cody that Dana hadn't been in the explosion, or that Fontenot had taken her.

He didn't want to hand Cody the hope that she was alive, only to jerk his foundation out from under him by telling him she was Fontenot's captive. Dev had seen firsthand what Fontenot was capable of. He didn't want to think about what that might mean for Dana.

He sighed heavily and got out of the car. The borrowed deputy was leaning back against the hotel door, balancing on two legs of his straight-backed chair.

Dev unceremoniously kicked the chair out from under him.

The deputy tumbled to the ground and scrambled up again immediately, looking angry until he saw who it was. Then he straightened up, jammed his hat back down on his head and said, "Evening, sir."

"Any problems?"

"No sir."

"Fine. Dismissed." Dev stuck his key into the lock.
"Uh, sir?"

Dev whirled around, satisfied to see the look of abject terror on the face of the young deputy sheriff.

He had that effect on people. He liked it. "Well?"

"Uh, he got room service a little while ago. That was okay, wasn't it?"

Dev blew out a breath between his teeth. "Did he knock you out with the water pitcher and tie you up with napkins and make his escape?"

The deputy grinned reluctantly. "No, sir."

"Dismissed." Dev turned back to the door, a vague uneasiness settling under his breastbone. He wouldn't have expected Cody to rouse himself enough to want room service, unless...

"Ah, hell!" Dev let himself in, and cursed.

Just as he feared, the room reeked of bourbon. Cody sat at the little table with a glass and a bottle in front of him. The bottle was about a third empty.

Cody was a pathetic sight, with his handcuffed, bandaged hands, and his T-shirt and jeans covered in soot and mud. He had a scrape on his cheek and a dark bruise on his left jaw where Dev had coldcocked him. His face was drawn and streaked with soot and tears.

He looked like death, with the skin stretched taut across his pale cheekbones and those astounding blue eyes shining glassily. His hair was messy, like a lunatic's, and his nose and the corners of his mouth looked pinched.

As Dev watched, Cody lifted the glass to his lips with an unsteady, bandaged hand. His other hand had to follow because of the handcuffs. As he drank, Cody's dull gaze focused on Dev's face.

''You goddamn ugly swamp rat,'' Cody said conversationally, his words slow and just barely slurred.

''Nice to see you, too,'' Dev said as Cody continued to swallow bourbon. ''You drunk?''

Cody shook his head tiredly. ''Unfortunately, no. Not at all.'' Cody drained the glass and filled it again, his movements uncharacteristically clumsy as he tried to manipulate with the handcuffs. ''Only my fingertips are numb.''

''Too bad.'' Dev sat down across from his friend.

Cody looked up at Dev, his eyes like blue burning coals in his haunted face. ''Yeah, it's just too damn bad, ain't it? I only have two thirds of a bottle left. I figure that'll get me up to about my knuckles, then you're going to have to go get me some more.''

''Maybe we should find another swamp rat, one that makes his own.''

''Couldn't be any worse than this rotgut.'' Cody reached for the bottle, forgetting the handcuffs. He almost knocked it over.

Dev reached out and righted the bottle with one hand, and dug the keys to the handcuffs from his pocket with the other.

''Let me get those off you.'' He avoided Cody's eyes as he unlocked the cuffs, not that it did any good. He could still feel his partner's anguished, bewildered gaze.

He pulled the bottle toward him, but Cody grabbed it.

''You slimy swamp snake. If I could move I'd kill you. What the hell's wrong with you? Why wouldn't you let me save her? I could have saved her. You son of a bitch! Why?'' Cody's red-rimmed eyes brimmed over with tears.

Dev hadn't been moved by many things in his life, but the sight of his best friend so hurt, so angry, so helpless, almost made him cry. He had to swallow a couple of times before he could talk.

"I was just trying to protect you, my man," he said. "You'd have killed yourself in that inferno."

"So?" Cody's shoulders slumped and he began tracing patterns in the condensation on the table. "So what if I burned up? What the hell difference would it have made to anybody? What difference have I ever made? Not good for nothing but making Dana's life miserable." His face drained of what little color was left in it and he looked up at Dev.

"Dana?" His voice was tentative, hopeless.

Dev looked at his friend, wondering how to tell him. Damn, he wished Cody would pass out. The boy had been given enough morphine to choke a swamp gator, and he'd poured quite a bit of bourbon in on top of it. It would be much easier in the morning when Cody's head was clearer and Dev's brain was rested.

"Dev? What did you f-find? You've been out there, haven't you? Do they know anything yet?" Cody took a long, shuddering breath and flexed a bandaged hand. "It's probably too soon, isn't it? You know, I think my knuckles are finally getting numb."

Cody smiled, the expression looking eerie on his devastated, ravaged face. "That's good. I'm looking forward to it moving on up my arms." He looked down at himself, then up at Dev, and the tears in his eyes spilled down his cheeks.

"You know what, Dev? Liquor can numb some things. It can numb your brain, your fingers, maybe even your soul."

He fisted his right hand and slammed it into his

chest, again and again. "But nothing," he said in time with his self-inflicted blows. "Nothing—ever—stops—the pain—here."

The tears were running down his face and his eyes had turned to a dull slate gray. He hammered at his chest with his fist. "It—never—ever—stops."

Finally he let his arms fall limp to the table and bent his head, staring at his hands. "What happened, Dev? Was it—quick? Oh, God, the bedroom went last. I saw it. She was in the bedroom, wasn't she? She knew. She had to have heard the explosion. She knew she was going to die. I never should have left her."

Dev put his hand over Cody's. He grimaced, blinking rapidly, searching inside himself for the cool detachment that made him a good detective.

"Cody…" Dev started, but Cody wasn't listening. He pulled away and buried his head in his bandaged hands.

"Cody." Dev pulled his hands away from his face. "Listen to me."

"Go away and let me drink myself to death." Cody reached for the bottle, but Dev retrieved it easily.

Cody shrugged and rubbed his palm across his cheeks, smearing the dirt and soot.

"Listen to me," Dev said again. "There are no human remains in the house." Dev's heart wrenched as he watched comprehension slowly dawn in his friend's face.

"No r-remains?"

Dev shook his head. "None."

Cody looked at his hands, then at Dev. He wiped his face again and squeezed his eyes shut as he pushed his tangled, sweat-damp hair back from his forehead.

Dev watched the progress of Cody's thoughts on

his expressive face. The slow understanding that Dana wasn't dead, then the dawning realization of what that meant. But it took a lot longer for Cody's drugged brain to reach the same conclusion Dev had.

"She's alive."

The choked, joyous words cut through Dev like a hot knife through butter.

"She's alive. Oh, God, she's alive." The sobs shook his bowed shoulders.

But then the joy on his ravaged face turned to abject horror. "Fontenot's got her," he muttered. His bandaged hands curled into fists and he slammed them down on the table. "We got to go, Dev. What the hell we sitting around here for?"

Cody threw himself up out of the chair, then swayed and almost fell. Dev jumped up and caught him just in time.

"Not tonight, Code. Tonight you got to rest."

"Hell, no," Cody slurred, trying to wrench himself out of Dev's grasp. But Dev held on, dismayed by how weak and clumsy his partner was.

Dev bodily threw Cody on the bed and waited, but Cody didn't launch himself up again. Dev relaxed a bit, sitting back on his haunches next to the bed.

His partner seemed to have gone to sleep, or passed out. It didn't matter which. Dev breathed a sigh of relief, watching his friend for a minute as the lines of pain and grief on his face smoothed out a little.

Dev had never loved a woman like that. He knew all about physical pain, but not since he was a child had he ever let anybody close enough to him to hurt him. He'd never loved a woman as much as Cody loved Dana.

The only two people Dev had cared about in a long,

long time were Cody and Thibaud Johnson, his mentor. And Thibaud was dead.

Dev loved Cody. He hurt for him. He ached to make things right for his partner, but there was nothing he could do.

After making sure Cody was unconscious but breathing normally, Devereaux Gautier stood abruptly and slammed out of the motel room. He paced up and down in front of the door for a few minutes, his thoughts in turmoil, his heart heavy. Then he turned toward the stucco wall and slammed his fist again and again into it, wishing with every blow that the solid brick was Fontenot's face.

Cody was right. It never, ever stopped hurting.

FONTENOT FINISHED splicing the wires into the household circuit at Dana Maxwell's apartment. He took a last, scrutinizing look at the magnetic door locks he'd installed on her front and back doors. Then he flipped the switch. A dull thud told him the magnets were working properly.

Stepping over to the front door, he pulled on it, exerting as much force as he could. The door held. He pulled a small black remote control unit from his pocket. He pressed a button. The resulting thud made him smile. He turned the knob and the door opened smoothly.

Perfect. Let the police try to get past that. Of course, the magnetic locks were only a last resort. If he stayed calm and focused, Maxwell would play right into his hands, and the police wouldn't have to be involved.

If everything went as planned, Mrs. Maxwell would be the one directly responsible for her husband's death, and Fontenot would be out of the country before the police ever got involved.

Slipping the remote control back into his pocket, Fontenot went into the bedroom.

"Mrs. Maxwell? Mrs. Maxwell." He touched the side of her face and she jerked.

"I do apologize for leaving you bound all night. I know it must be dreadfully uncomfortable." He grabbed the blanket and pulled her upright, pushing her legs off the bed and leaving her in a sitting position.

Her green eyes flashed at him like lasers. He chuckled. "It is a good thing looks can't kill. I have a feeling I would be much the worse for wear if they could." He pulled a razor-sharp switchblade from his pocket and cut the taped blanket away.

"Don't tense up, Mrs. Maxwell. And certainly, I hope you realize it would not be a good idea for you to challenge me physically." He held up the knife. "As you see, this is a very well-honed blade. It could easily slip between your ribs, or slice quite a deep cut in, say, your cheek."

Her quick, alarmed glance at the knife assured him that she understood the gravity of her situation. He held the weapon in front of her face as he pressed the mechanism that caused it to close with a snicking sound. Sliding it back into his side pocket, he reached behind him where, securely tucked into his belt, was a Glock. He brandished it in front of her face.

"And of course, just in case you decide to run..." Smiling serenely, he inspected the polished surface of the gun, then wiped an imaginary smudge off the barrel and slipped it back into his belt.

"Shall we give you a reprieve from that nasty

tape?'' He ripped the tape off her mouth in one swift motion, which left her gasping.

"You sick ghoul," she hissed. "Don't you know you can't get away with this? The entire New Orleans Police Department will be on top of you in no time."

"Oh, please, Mrs. Maxwell. Don't insult my intelligence and your own. As soon as I've set everything up here, I shall be on my way to a nonextradition country, where I have had accommodations set up and waiting for me for a long time. Your dedicated husband interrupted my departure last time, which is why he ended up getting himself shot. I hope he has more sense than to try to sneak in reinforcements this time. He should realize that he will be jeopardizing your life as well as his own."

"However Cody does it, he *will* stop you, and lock you up where you belong. And if he doesn't do it, I will. You can't just play with people's lives and get away with it."

Fontenot laughed in genuine amusement. "Why, Mrs. Maxwell, of course I can. I've been doing it for years."

Chapter Fifteen

Dana stared at the madman who had kidnapped her. She had never been so frightened in her life. He was totally insane, but the tone of his voice, his movements, seemed completely rational. And he truly believed he was superior to everyone else in the world.

"You're a madman, Fontenot, and somehow, Cody will prove it. It's just a matter of time. They'll get you. I only hope you get to suffer as much as you've made others suffer. Or more."

Fontenot shook his head regretfully and held up the piece of tape he'd ripped off her mouth. "I would hate to have to tape your mouth again," he said. "It appears the tape irritates your sensitive skin. But if you can't carry on a decent conversation, I'm afraid it will be necessary."

Looking at the duct tape, Dana noticed for the first time the burning sensation around her mouth. It felt like a layer of skin had been ripped off with the tape.

Her heart raced in apprehension as she eyed Fontenot and his strip of tape. As much as she wanted to curse and rail at him, she knew she needed to remain calm and rational, and as free of restraint as possible.

She had to stop him, and she wouldn't have a prayer if she were bound and gagged again.

"Please," she said placatingly. "Don't tape my mouth again. That hurt so badly. I'll stay calm." She did her best not to allow her distaste to show on her face.

Fontenot smiled at her. "You are a brave and clever one, aren't you?" He chuckled. "You amuse me, Mrs. Maxwell. Now…" He grabbed her arm and pulled her to her feet.

Dana swayed slightly. Inactivity and lack of water made her feel weak and light-headed. "Could I have some water, please?"

Fontenot grabbed her by her upper arms and shook her. "Do not faint on me," he said, shaking her roughly. The pain from his fingers digging into her upper arms overrode the dizziness.

"Women!" he spat. "You can ruin anything. Now, get in here." He guided her roughly into the living room and pushed her down on the couch.

He disappeared for an instant, then returned with a glass of tap water. "Drink this, quickly. Because I need you to perform a little chore for me."

After draining the glass, Dana rubbed her arms, where red marks were already forming.

Fontenot grabbed the portable phone and pushed it into her hands. "Please telephone your husband, Mrs. Maxwell. It is time for him to come here."

"Go to hell," she responded.

She saw the flash of Fontenot's pinkie ring just before she felt it graze her cheek as he struck her.

CODY STRAIGHTENED, arching his back and stretching. He'd been crouched down for most of the morning, sorting through the burned rubble that had been the lake house.

He'd found bits and pieces of their belongings. Nothing much. Most of it had been either blown apart or burned.

Some time later he might be saddened by the loss of the place that had held so many good memories for Dana and him, but right now all he wanted was a clue. Something, anything that would tell him where Fontenot had taken Dana. He was beginning to think he wasn't going to find it here.

His brain was still dazed from the day before and all he'd gone through. Cody had seen some dreadful things in his career as a police detective, but the fact that he'd watched others suffer didn't lessen his awe that a human being could survive the horror he'd experienced when he'd thought Dana was dead.

Right now, just thinking about it made him weak and sick with terror and grief.

But she was alive. She was alive and he had to believe she was safe. If Fontenot was true to form, he wouldn't do anything to her without Cody there to see it. That wasn't Fontenot's style. He didn't enjoy the physical torture nearly as much as he enjoyed the emotional and mental anguish he inflicted.

Cody clenched his bandaged fists, ignoring the pain from his burns. Fontenot would suffer for what he'd done to them. If Cody had anything to say about it, Fontenot would suffer.

Cody looked around and saw Dev climbing the hill toward the house. Good. Cody was ready for some action. He couldn't find any clues here.

"Dev! Let's get out of here," he shouted. Maybe if they went back to New Orleans, they could trace

Fontenot's steps, try to figure out where he might have gone.

The bigger man shrugged. "And go where, my man?"

Cody threw down the stick he'd been using to poke through the rubble and carefully dusted his bandaged hands together. The burns were only first-degree, with a couple of blisters, but they hurt like hell, all the time. "I don't know. Back to the precinct, maybe. What I can't figure out is why he hasn't contacted me."

Cody pushed his hair back off his forehead with his forearm. "Am I missing something, Dev?"

"Take a look over here," Dev said, walking carefully toward the spot where the back door had been.

Cody followed him, with a last glance toward the bedroom, trying to quell the memory of those endless seconds when the whole place had been engulfed in flame.

Dana hadn't been in there. She was safe. She had to be.

Dev walked about a hundred yards away from the house, toward the wooded area. Cody followed him, glancing back at the place where the house was, measuring the distance with his eye. "What's going on, Dev? What have you found?"

Dev stopped and crouched down. "Look here."

Cody crouched next to Dev, searching the ground with his gaze. The grass and weeds were flattened and bruised, as if someone had walked there, sat there. And not just one person. The signs indicated that two people had been there. There were a couple of places where it was obvious a small foot had slipped on damp grass.

Cody touched the flattened grass, then twisted

around to look back at the house. Slowly, the truth dawned in his still-hazy brain. "He had her here, didn't he, Dev? This is far enough from the house to be safe from the explosion. The bastard had her here, held her here. If he's hurt her, Dev..."

"Take it easy, Code. You said yourself, he needs her alive, to get to you."

"Yeah...." Cody wasn't reassured. As he well knew, the human body could take a lot, and still remain alive. *Bastard.*

"I swear, if he's harmed one hair on her head..." A wave of helpless fury washed over him.

After one more quick glance around, he stood, looking down the hill to where he and Dev had been standing when the house exploded. "They watched."

Dev looked up at him. "Huh?"

"Look down there. Don't you see? Look at this vantage point. It's perfect. They could see us, but we'd be hard-pressed to spot them." His fury mounted. "He made her watch while the house exploded. She saw everything." Cody whirled and started back toward the wreckage of the house. "Come on, Dev. We've got to get back to New Orleans."

"Wait a minute." Dev followed Cody. "Mind giving me some explanation here?"

Cody talked as he walked. "Okay. You know most of it. But here goes. First he leaves things for me. Nice things. No threats, nothing tricky. A cup of my favorite coffee on my desk. Takes my newspaper from in front of my door and leaves it in my car."

As he made his way down the hill with Dev beside him, Cody outlined what Fontenot had done, and as he did, anger and determination settled cold and hard in his chest.

Somehow, he would make Fontenot pay for what he'd done to Dana and to him. "It's like he feeds on emotions, Dev. He put Dana's earring on my car seat, knowing I'd understand his message. He could get to her. That's what he was telling me. Then he rigged that gun—not to kill me. In fact he didn't even mean for me to get shot." Cody heard the bitterness in his voice.

"Too slow."

"What?" Cody turned to look at Dev, bewildered by his words.

"That's what Dana said when she saw the booby trap. She said you'd been too slow."

Cody stared at Dev. Dana had said the same thing to him. *She understood.* She'd figured out what Fontenot had been doing.

"Too slow is right. I should have sensed that the trap was there. Then he rigs the lights in Dana's car to look like an explosion. He was watching, Dev. Just like up there." Cody gestured back up the hill. "See? It's exactly like I said. You can't even see that spot from here. But they could see us. He made Dana watch. She had to watch me trying to get to her." Cody's voice broke.

He shuddered as revulsion for Fontenot rose in his throat like bile. His chest hurt with anguished sympathy for what his *chère* had gone through. She'd had to live those same endless seconds he'd lived as he'd watched the house blow up, as he'd thought she was burning up in the explosion.

A fierce, hot urge to kill Fontenot with his bare hands raged inside Cody. He wanted to rip the man's heart out.

"He deserves to die," Dev remarked.

Cody glanced at his partner, a realization dawning inside him. "No. That's where you're wrong. A man like Fontenot, who lives on other people's pain, deserves worse than death." Cody brushed the tips of his fingers over the cold steel of his revolver. "Much as I'd like to blow him away, he doesn't deserve that kind of clean, quick death. What that bastard hates more than anything is that he wasn't smart enough to stay out of prison. That's why he's so obsessed with me, because I put him in prison. I locked him up."

They reached the car, and Cody turned to Dev. "And that's what I'm going to do again. If it's the last thing I ever do, I'll lock Fontenot away." Cody took a long breath. "I'll get that maniac off the street, so Dana can be safe again."

Cody's cell phone rang. "That's probably Hamilton, wondering where we are. I'll tell you something else, Dev," he said, pointing the phone at his partner. "I'm not letting Dana go again, either. I've wasted too much time already. I'll take a desk job first."

Dev grinned and gave Cody a double thumbs-up as he pressed the button on the cell phone.

"Maxwell," he said.

"Cody?"

His heart leapt in his chest, sending adrenaline pumping through him. "Dana? *Chère?*" His voice broke and he grabbed the phone with both hands. He'd known she was alive, somewhere. He'd prayed she was safe, but the low, sweet sound of her voice made him realize how afraid he'd been that he would never hear her say his name again. That he would never hold her again. That he'd never have the chance to make up to her for not keeping her safe.

His pulse hammered like a piston, and his throat

grew tight. He felt tears pricking his eyes as he took a long breath and tried to make his voice sound calm. If Fontenot had her, she wasn't safe yet. "Where are you *chère?* I've been worried."

"Cody, are you all right?"

He closed his eyes. "Sure. I'm fine. What about you?" Such mundane words to convey such intense relief.

"Cody, come home, please."

There was a slight tremor in her voice, like she got when she was pleading a case. Cody was sure nobody had ever noticed it but him. But then he knew her so well. He knew every nuance, every tiny breath she took and what it meant.

Cody's heart was full to overflowing with helpless love for his brave wife.

He forced a cheerfulness into his voice. "Hey, *chère,* I'm on my way. You at home? Are you okay? What happened?"

She took a shaky breath. He waited, wondering if Fontenot was listening, wondering what he should say. He probably should act as naturally as possible, ask the questions any man would ask under the circumstances. He gripped the phone tighter, afraid of saying the wrong thing, afraid any wrong word or sound would put her in more danger.

"*Chère,* has Fontenot got you? Did he hurt you?"

"No, I'm okay," she murmured, then she gasped again quietly. "I just want to see you."

"Me, too, *chère,* me, too." For a moment, Cody's love and fear overrode his cop's judgment. "I thought you were dead, *chère,*" he said, not caring if Fontenot was listening, not caring if the man heard the tears in his voice.

"Oh, Cody, I know. I'm so sorry."

"No, *chère,* don't be sorry. What happened? Come on, talk to me."

"He dragged me out of the house, Cody," she said, her voice sounding tinny over the phone. She sounded like she was about to cry. Cody clenched his jaw and changed his mind about locking Fontenot away. Maybe he *would* kill him with his bare hands.

"He made me watch the house blow up. Oh, Cody, you thought I was in there. I'm so sorry." Her voice was getting a hysterical edge to it. She sounded as if she was about to break down. If Fontenot was there, he was certainly enjoying this.

"It's okay. Everything's okay. I'm just glad to hear your voice." Cody swallowed hard, trying to stop the emotions clogging his throat. "Tell me what happened."

"He just…just threw me in a car and drove and drove and drove, then he s-said he was going after you and he tossed me out of the car."

Cody frowned. That didn't sound like the diabolical maniac he knew. What was going on? He was more convinced than ever that Fontenot was there with Dana, making her say these things.

"So I caught a cab home. Cody, I'm scared. Will you come home?"

Cody's heart twisted painfully in his chest. He felt so helpless, so impotent. Fontenot had his wife, and he was powerless to save her. "I'll be there. But you promise me you're okay? Is Fontenot there?"

"No," she said quickly. "I told you, he dumped me out of the car. But I'm fine. I just want to see you. I really need you to come home, safe and sound."

"Me, too, *chère.* You're at your apartment? I'll be

there within two hours, okay?'' He looked around and caught Dev's eye and motioned for him. ''Where did he dump you out?''

''In uh—Algiers.''

Cody's anger began to flare again. Had Fontenot really done that, dumped her out in Algiers, where some of the roughest neighborhoods in New Orleans were? Cody didn't buy it. Fontenot wouldn't let Dana out of his sight. She was his trump card.

''But you're okay?''

''I'm fine,'' she said shakily. ''I promise. But one thing, Cody.''

''Yeah?'' he said, his heart thumping harder in his chest.

''Bring me a surprise, okay? Like you always do?'' Dana's voice became a little stronger, a trace more determined. ''Don't forget.''

''Dana—'' he started, but the line went dead. ''Damn!'' What the hell was that last about? Dana hated surprises. *Don't forget.*

Dev walked up. ''What is it, my man? You look sick.''

Cody shook his head, staring at the phone for a moment before he put it back in its case. ''Dana.'' He realized he was shaking when he had trouble getting the phone into its belt holder.

Don't forget. He hadn't forgotten her words in the pirogue. *I don't like surprises. Promise me you'll never surprise me.*

''That was Dana? Is she okay?''

Cody shook his head. ''No, she's not. She's at her apartment, and Fontenot's there. He's got her, and he's using her as bait to lure me to him.''

''She told you all that?''

Cody nodded, and smiled, pride and admiration for his wife swelling in his chest. "Yeah. She sure did."

DANA COULDN'T LET GO of the phone. Fontenot had cut the connection, but she still gripped it as if it were Cody's hands.

"What was that about a surprise?" he said harshly, wrenching the phone out of her numbed hands.

She looked at him in distaste, touching the cut on her cheek where his pinkie ring had scratched her. She lifted her chin. "I always ask Cody to bring me a surprise. You warned me not to make him suspicious. He'd be suspicious if I hadn't mentioned that." She swallowed. "He should be here within two hours."

"Well, you did sound very natural and fairly calm. I hope you managed to convince him. If he doesn't come alone, things could get very messy. It would be a shame to have to kill more people than necessary."

Dana glared at Fontenot, hoping the mixture of terror and relief washing through her didn't show on her face. Had her pitiful attempt at warning Cody worked? Would Cody remember her saying she hated surprises? At the time, Cody had been irritated at her. He'd fired back at her that she didn't like to have fun. If he didn't remember, if he failed to understand her vague message... It was hard for her to even formulate the thought, although it lay there in her brain like a rock balanced precariously over a town, ominous, hovering, ever-present. Fontenot would kill Cody.

"Now, Mrs. Maxwell," he said, consulting his watch. "If it takes your dear husband two hours or so to get here, we have a bit of a wait ahead of us. Why don't you make us some coffee?"

"Why don't you drop dead?"

"COME ON. CAN'T YOU MOVE any faster?" Cody stood motionless, waiting for the technical guys to finish taping the wires to his chest.

"Stay cool, Code."

If Cody hadn't been so worried about Dana, he'd be enjoying the heck out of Dev's unease. The big, black-haired detective paced up and down, up and down, his hands shoved in the back pockets of his jeans, his bearded face dark with worry.

But as it was, Dev's concern only emphasized the gravity of the situation.

"Ouch!" he exclaimed as one of the technicians ripped off a piece of tape.

Captain Hamilton came in and clasped him on the shoulder. "You sure about this, Maxwell?"

He nodded. "Absolutely. Fontenot is capable of anything. I've got to go in there alone. You guys can't make a move until I'm sure he's totally focused on me. He'll kill her, Captain." His heart felt as though it was tearing in two as he spoke those words.

"He'll kill you."

Cody shook his head. "I can take care of myself. But if he gets a whiff of police, she's dead." He cleared his throat. "Please wait, captain. Wait until the last possible minute. And remember, the bastard loves booby traps. He'll have something on the door."

"You just make sure that wire stays in place, because if we lose touch, we'll have no choice but to use force."

"Excuse me, Captain Hamilton. Detective Maxwell, can you turn around? I need to attach the transmitter to your side, under your arm." The young man held up the apparatus.

Cody looked down, where strips of tape ran down

his chest and belly like lines painted on a highway. He touched a couple of the strips of tape to be sure they were secure. He knew wearing a wire was necessary, but something nagged at him. Fontenot was sure to suspect a wire. The man wouldn't miss something as simple as that. Dana's safety depended on Cody getting a confession out of Fontenot quickly. He knew a simple kidnapping charge wouldn't stop the man. He'd be out of prison again in no time, *if* they even got a conviction. No, if he couldn't put Fontenot away for his wife's murder, they'd never be safe.

God, please help me. I can't lose her again.

"This microphone is supersensitive." Captain Hamilton gestured toward the wires. "It's state of the art, and very expensive. So try not to break it."

Cody smiled wryly at the captain's lame attempt at humor. "Do my best, sir."

Hamilton cleared his throat. "Well, I'm sure you will."

"Sir?" The technician needed Cody's attention. "The transmitter needs to go up high under your arm. Would you like me to shave your armpit?"

A snort from behind him told Cody that Dev was confident enough to laugh at his situation. Cody half turned and sent Dev a well-known and unmistakable gesture, before he shook his head shortly at the technician.

Dev chuckled, clasped Cody around the back of his neck and gave him a quick, awkward hug. "We'll be ready, Code. Just say the word and we'll be in there in two seconds."

"Thanks, Dev."

"She'll be okay, my man. You two belong together."

Cody nodded, then blinked to rid his eyes of hazy tears.

"That's it, sir."

Cody winced as the tape pulled at the hair under his arm. "Thanks," he said wryly as he dressed.

"Okay, men, let's get out there and get that son of a bitch," the captain said.

Cody started out the door, still worried about Fontenot finding the wire. "Hold it."

"What's the matter, Code?" Dev said. "Change your mind about that shave?"

Cody shot Dev a look, then gestured to the technician. "Captain, give me a minute. I've got an idea."

CODY TRIED THE APARTMENT DOOR. Sure enough it was unlocked. He shook his head. Fontenot was so sure of himself. He'd gotten either real cocky or real desperate. Cody profoundly hoped Fontenot was desperate, because if he didn't hold all the cards, he certainly held the trump. He had Dana.

They still had no concrete evidence that Fontenot was behind anything that had happened, except Dana's kidnapping, and that wasn't enough. Cody wanted to get him for the murder of his wife, so he'd have to goad him into confessing.

He rubbed his chest, where the wire was taped as he stepped into Dana's living room. The tape itched like hell and pulled at his chest hairs.

The first thing Cody saw was his wife, sitting on the couch, curled up with her feet under her, holding a magazine with white-knuckled fingers. When he stepped into the room, she looked up, abject terror on her face.

Cody's throat tightened with emotion.

"Dana," he whispered. The relief that coursed through him when he saw her almost undid him. She was pale, and terrified, and there was a bruise and a scratch on her cheek, but she was here, in front of him, alive.

"Cody." Her voice was uncertain and small. She stood up, clutching the magazine, wrinkling its pages in her hands.

Come on chère, *play out the charade. Don't quit on me now.* He tried to send her reassuring signals without letting any emotion show on his face.

"Oh, Cody," she breathed, but she didn't move.

"It's okay, *chère*," he soothed. He hated the bastard for setting them up like this, for watching as he saw Dana for the first time since those awful moments when the house had blown up.

"I thought you were dead. My God, let me look at you." He took her hands, which were icy cold, and held them tightly as he looked at her. Cody forced himself not to look around, to keep his gaze riveted on Dana. He stepped toward her, the hairs on the back of his neck prickling, knowing Fontenot was watching them, feeding on their emotions. The ghoul must be satiated by now, he thought. He squeezed her hands. "I'm glad you're safe."

Her eyes began to fill with tears, and he nodded slightly. He knew what she was thinking. *Not safe. Never safe.* Unless he could keep his cool. He had to act like a husband who's just found out his wife was alive. He couldn't just grab her and hold her so close they'd meld into one person the way he wanted to do.

His job was to perform in front of Fontenot and a large number of NOPD detectives, the assistant district attorney and a couple of U.S. marshals.

He let go of her hands and held out his arms. She hesitated. It couldn't have been more than a split second, but he saw it and felt it. His heart pounded in apprehension. *Come on* chère, *perform for them.*

He grinned at her. "Come here," he said. "I've got a surprise for you."

Relief flooded her face and she flung herself into his arms. She knew what his words meant. She knew he was telling her he'd understood her cryptic message.

Cody hoped Fontenot was positioned behind her, hoped he hadn't seen the joy and relief on her face. It took every last ounce of his strength to keep his own face from showing what he was thinking right now.

Touching her, Cody gave himself up for an instant to the overwhelming relief and love that engulfed him as he held her.

He'd watched her die, and yet she was alive. Holding her moved him more than anything that had ever happened to him in his entire life. He couldn't help it. He had to speak, Fontenot and his evil intent be damned.

"Dana, my *chère.* You are my foundation. You're my reason for living. When I thought you were dead, I thought I would die." He pulled her tighter.

He was awed by the depth of his love for her, humbled by the gratitude he felt toward God for keeping her safe. She was warm, whole, alive. And she was in his arms. "Whatever happens," he whispered in her ear, "I got to hold you again."

Chapter Sixteen

I got to hold you again.

Cody's words made Dana want to cry. "Hold me tight," she breathed, burrowing her face into Cody's shoulder. For an instant, she gave into her weakness and pretended they were safe. She knew she was being foolish, but she'd just had to hold him, touch him, just this one more time. "Tighter. You're here. You came for me."

He pushed her back and looked at her face. *"Chère?* You okay?" Gently, he touched the cut on her cheek and a frown marred his features.

She smiled at him shakily. "Now I am," she said. "Now that you're here. Oh, Cody, I'm so scared."

"Isn't this special," Fontenot said from behind her. She stiffened, and felt Cody go rigid in her arms. For an instant, despite his mention of the surprise, she was terrified that Cody hadn't understood her message, that he wasn't ready for Fontenot. Before he pushed her away, he covered her hand with his and brushed it across his chest.

A wire. He was wearing a wire.

She'd seen him wired for sound before. How many times had she rubbed ointment into the tape burns on his chest from wearing a wire so the police could hear incriminating conversations?

He was wired. The police were outside listening. Dana's knees felt watery from relief. But they weren't out of the woods yet.

The good guys were outside. She and Cody were inside with a monster.

Cody gently set her aside, and she let him.

"Fontenot." Cody's voice was icy.

"Detective Maxwell, how kind of you to join us."

Dana clenched her teeth at the irritating sound of the man's voice. She'd lived with that voice droning in her head for the past twenty-four hours. It frightened her to realize how easily, and without regret, she could rip out his throat.

"Your wife and I have had a lovely time."

Cody glanced at Dana, looked her up and down. She saw his eyes go dark and dangerous as they lit on the finger-shaped bruises on her wrists and arms. She nodded, and smiled shakily, hoping to assure him she was all right.

Relief mixed with cold fury on his face. It still awed her how much he cared. Her eyes burned. He loved her.

Cody Maxwell loved her.

Fontenot spoke conversationally. "I had a little trouble convincing her to call you. She had some ridiculous notion of sacrificing herself to save you, but I...twisted her arm, so to speak." Fontenot smiled his eerie smile, and Dana resisted the urge to rub her aching arm where he had indeed twisted it. She saw Cody's hands clench into fists.

"I assured her that it would be a waste of her lovely young life," Fontenot continued, "since I would certainly track you down, anyway, for putting me in prison and ruining my life.''

''You belong in prison, you piece of—''

''Now, Detective Maxwell. Why don't you just sit over there in that chair. You know I don't belong in prison. Why should I be in prison? Surely you jest. I've done nothing wrong.''

''You killed your wife, and you tried to kill me, and now you've added kidnapping.''

Fontenot shook his head and gestured toward the chair with his gun. ''Please have a seat, Detective Maxwell. Make yourself comfortable.''

Dana watched the scene with ever-deepening horror. Every word he spoke, every gesture he made, convinced her more and more that Fontenot was certifiably insane.

He had a sick obsession with Cody. She could see it in his glittering eyes. She could hear it in the self-satisfied tone of his voice.

How could the police possibly get in here before he killed Cody? She glanced at the front door. He hadn't locked it!

Fontenot laughed. ''Oh, thank you for the reminder, Mrs. Maxwell. But I assure you I haven't forgotten about the door.'' He put his hand in his pocket and pulled out the remote control. He pressed the button and Dana heard the ominous thud that indicated that the door had locked. ''Detective Maxwell, you might be interested to know that the door is now electronically locked with a magnet, which exerts two thousand pounds of force. Clever?''

Dana frowned. He'd made the door practically impenetrable, but what about the windows?

Fontenot smiled at her. ''You're wondering about

the windows, aren't you, Mrs. Maxwell? See those little wires on each of them? I can assure you, if anyone tries to open or break them, they'll be in for quite an explosive surprise.''

Dismay flooded her. What would Cody do? How could they win against this maniac?

''Mrs. Maxwell, would you be kind enough to take these distasteful devices and cuff your husband's hands behind his back?''

''No, I will not,'' she said, but when she glanced at Cody he nodded, a dark intensity shining in his blue eyes.

With trembling hands, Dana took the handcuffs and did as she was told.

''Cody, I can't do this,'' she said, her eyes blurry with tears. ''He's going to kill you.''

''Mrs. Maxwell, I'd advise you to, and quickly.'' The silky voice had an edge to it, an edge of something—maybe hysteria?

''Go ahead, Dana. It's okay,'' Cody said, his voice soothing her. ''Don't worry about it.''

''I'm glad you're seeing reason, Detective Maxwell. After all, I've never done anything, isn't that right?''

Dana looked at Fontenot, hearing the note of triumph in his voice as he spoke each word carefully and clearly. Did he know about the wire? Was their last possible chance for freedom gone?

She saw in the man's eyes that he knew. He gestured toward her with the gun.

''Move away, Mrs. Maxwell. I need to check on something.''

He pushed Cody against the wall, and Dana winced as Cody almost lost his footing. She reached out for him, but checked herself when she saw the warning look in his eyes.

"Aha," Fontenot said, "Just as I thought." He smiled at Cody. "As I said, Detective Maxwell, you know I'm an innocent man, don't you? I served my time for my regrettable lapse of reason in shooting you. It was an act of desperation I was forced to because of your demented pursuit of me."

With no change of expression, Fontenot flipped open his switchblade and slit Cody's shirt and T-shirt. Dana couldn't contain a moan as the tip of the knife nicked his beautiful, golden skin and a drop of blood welled up.

"Tsk, tsk, tsk," Fontenot clucked. "Really, Detective. Did you think I wouldn't check?"

Cody glared at him and cursed under his breath.

Dana almost lost her last precarious hold on her own sanity. *Oh, Cody.*

Piece by piece, Fontenot jerked each strip of tape off Cody's chest.

Dana blinked, and two fat tears fell over her cheeks.

Cody kicked out and hit Fontenot in the knees. Fontenot crumpled and the gun went flying.

Dana dived for the gun as Fontenot grabbed Cody's legs and knocked him to the floor. Fontenot struggled to get up, while Cody lay ominously still.

"Stop it, Fontenot," Dana said, pointing the gun at him. "Get over there." She was amazed at her voice. She sounded calm, cold...mean.

That wasn't at all the way she felt. Her hands shook and her heart pounded. Sweat ran down her temples, while tears spilled down her cheeks.

She glanced at Cody, but he looked as though he

was unconscious. He must have hit his head. *Please be okay, Cody. Please.*

Then she turned her full attention on the madman. "Get over there!" she ground out between clenched teeth, as she nodded toward the other side of the room.

Fontenot rose, delicately rolling up the strips of tape and tossing them to the floor. Then he pulled each tiny wire out of the microphone, dropped it to the floor and stepped on it. A metallic crushing sound rent the air.

Fontenot seemed totally unconcerned that she was pointing a loaded weapon at him.

"There, now," he said softly. "That's taken care of." He turned around to look at Dana.

"Excuse me, Mrs. Maxwell? You were saying?"

Dana aimed the gun at his right eye, dismayed at the quiver in the barrel. Guns were much heavier than she'd realized. "I—if you don't move I'll shoot you in the eye."

He started to walk toward her.

"No!" she shouted. "I am serious. Do not give me any reason to pull this trigger, because I'm incredibly nervous right now." She gestured with the gun barrel. "Put your hands up. Do it or I'll shoot you right now."

"Mrs. Maxwell, if you shoot me it will be cold-blooded murder," Fontenot said serenely.

"I don't care," she said, licking dry lips and shaking her head.

Fontenot gave her an assessing look, as if he were judging the advisability of lunging at her and grabbing the gun, but she spread her legs apart and held the gun out in front of her with both hands, just as she'd seen cops on television do.

"Mrs. Maxwell, you're obviously under a lot of

stress,'' Fontenot said, his voice sounding strained, but he did move a few feet away from Cody.

"You bet your life I'm under a lot of stress. You made me watch, made Cody think I'd been killed. You deserve to die.'' She shuddered.

"I understand now, why Cody became a cop. I can see why he gets so much satisfaction out of bringing criminals to justice. Killing you will be a service to all mankind, and it will be my pleasure to do it.''

Fontenot nodded, humming softly.

"You're a sociopath, a sick man who doesn't belong in society.''

"Go ahead, Mrs. Maxwell. Kill me. Then you will spend the rest of your life in prison and your dear husband will have to live with that.'' Fontenot smiled that eerie smile. "That just might be revenge enough for me.''

"Dana.''

Dana nearly dropped the gun in surprise and relief. "Cody?'' she said, turning her head toward him but never taking her eyes off Fontenot.

"You know, he's right.''

"Are you okay, Cody?''

"I've got a major headache from hitting the edge of that table, but yeah, I'm okay. Why don't you get these handcuffs off me and give me the gun.''

She shook her head, watching Fontenot, who had taken a step toward her. "No. He tried to kill you, and he's put both of us through hell. He can't live. He's got to die. I can see now why you are so dedicated. Why you believe in your job so much. These people have to be stopped.''

Dana heard Cody struggling to stand. He came over to her. "*Chère,* we still don't have anything to go on.''

"Nothing to go on? He rigged that gun. He blew up the lake house. He *k-kidnapped* me." Her strength was wavering. The gun shook. What was Cody doing? It was as if he were taking Fontenot's side.

"We can't prove anything but the kidnapping. He'll be back out in no time."

"That's right, Mrs. Maxwell. You see, I am more intelligent, more devious, than you or your clever husband can possibly imagine. The most they could do is try me for kidnapping, and I really don't think I would have a hard time beating that one."

Dana felt like crying. She felt like emptying the gun into Fontenot's worthless body and damn the consequences. Had he really beaten them after all? "But what are we going to do?"

"You undo these handcuffs and give me the gun and we'll call the police."

Dana wavered, looking at Cody. His gaze was intense, as if he were willing her to read his mind.

Fontenot began to move forward again.

"No!" Dana turned her full attention back to him. "You can't get away with it. I'll shoot you right now. You murdered your wife with those stupid snakes...."

"I have no idea what you're talking about, Mrs. Maxwell."

"*Chère*, it's over," Cody coaxed. "Come on. I need you, and I sure don't want to have to visit you in prison. He's outsmarted me." He sighed and his shoulders slumped.

Fontenot's smile turned into a grin.

"There's just one thing I don't understand."

Fontenot's grin faded a bit as he stared at Cody. "What do you mean?"

Dana couldn't believe it. He was giving up. Worse,

he was talking with this madman as if they were standing together around the water cooler.

As she watched, Cody shrugged, and his mouth quirked in a wry grin. "It just seems to me you could have done a better job of…well. It doesn't matter now."

Fontenot frowned. "A better job of what, Detective?"

Cody shook his head as if bewildered. "If you're so smart, how could you get such a simple booby trap wrong?"

Fontenot looked surprised, then angry. "Wrong?"

Cody nodded. "Yeah. And the car bomb. That was a pretty dumb mistake. And then of course there's your footprint at the scene of the explosion. I don't think they'll have too much trouble placing you there."

Fontenot's face turned splotchy red and he curled his fingers like claws. With teeth bared, he growled at Cody. "You pathetic moron. You didn't get it, did you? You never, ever figured it out. You're just as stupid as the rest of them. I thought you were at least a marginally worthy adversary. God help me, I'm surrounded by idiots." Fontenot advanced, but Dana brandished her gun.

He waved a hand at her as if she were a particularly irritating fly.

"The booby trap, as you so eloquently put it, was never meant to kill you. It wasn't even supposed to wound you. But then I overestimated your intelligence, didn't I, Detective? Not to mention your reaction time. Obviously you were too stupid to notice the blatant warning signs. Any fool would have felt the resistance in the door and heard the hammer click.

And the 'car bomb.' Ha! That worked perfectly. It was *supposed* to be just lights. In fact everything worked perfectly.''

''Just like with your wife?''

Fontenot laughed. ''Of course just like with my wife. The woman was a fool. She was having an affair. Cheating on *me*. So the solution was obvious. Poor Edie had a heart condition. Congenital.''

''So you rigged the cat above the bed, with blood dripping onto her pillow.''

''It was her cat,'' Fontenot said serenely, with a wave of his hand. ''Perfect.''

''Then you filled the refrigerator with snakes? Didn't you realize the cold would slow the snakes' metabolism to practically zero?''

Fontenot snorted. ''Don't be ridiculous. Of course I did. That's why I turned the refrigerator off. And the snakes were harmless, but the point is, Edie was terrified of snakes. I had other ideas cooked up, in case her heart was too strong for the snake trick, but yes, you imbecile. I killed her. I was on the other side of town, and I killed her. And you couldn't prove it. You'll never prove it!''

''No,'' Cody said, ''you're right. You destroyed the wire. But what were you going to do with us? Why didn't you just kill me and get it over with?''

''Why, Detective, that wouldn't be fun at all. Now, your wife understands me. I do enjoy the pain. It's so—shall we say satisfying? I was playing with you, like a cat with a mouse. And then I was going to let you watch your dear wife die one more time, only this time it would be for real. Then, for my pièce de résistance, I was going to let you kill yourself with your own gun. It would be my greatest achievement.''

Dana felt adrenaline coursing through her. "You miserable subhuman piece of garbage. You don't deserve to ever see light again. I feel like blowing you straight to hell, right now."

He laughed. "Your language is straight out of police television dramas. Let me say this, in a language you will understand. You don't have the guts, Mrs. Maxwell."

"You have no idea. I've watched Cody, and now I understand. There's a satisfaction in taking scumbags like you off the street."

"Dana," Cody pleaded, "you'd have to live with his blood on your hands for the rest of your life. Believe me, it's not worth it."

"Of course it's worth it. You've devoted your life to police work. You know it's worth it." She dashed tears away with the back of one hand, then curled it around the gun again. Her arms were shaking with fatigue from holding the heavy pistol up. "It's why you do what you do."

"I've never killed anybody, Dana."

She almost dropped the gun in shock. She'd never, ever, in the entire time they'd been married, realized that. She'd just assumed, because he kept getting shot that he also shot other people.

"N-never? Oh, Cody."

"It's not the way I do things. We'll get him, *chère*. We'll get him and put him behind bars. He'd rather die than be put back in prison."

"Ah, but Detective Maxwell, that's the wonderful part of this scheme." Fontenot's voice once again held triumph and self-satisfaction. "You haven't won. You'll never win. I'll get out again. And I must warn you that I never forget. You ruined my life when you put me away. I killed my wife so I could be free, and I'll kill you for the sheer pleasure of it.''

"You know, Fontenot? Unlike you, I do forget sometimes, which is why I like to carry a second wire in case the first one gets lost. Thank you for being so honest with us.''

Fontenot's face flamed and the veins stood out in his temples. He screamed—an inhuman sound, and dived for Cody, whose hands were still cuffed behind him.

Dana watched in horror as Fontenot attacked her husband. She pointed the gun. She closed her finger over the trigger.

I've never killed anybody, Dana. She shook her head to rid herself of Cody's voice. She had to do something. Fontenot still had the switchblade. He would kill Cody.

Dimly, in the background, she heard a huge crash as the police tried to break the door down, but Fontenot's magnetic lock held fast.

Crying, sobbing, she watched Fontenot's hands close around Cody's throat. "Stop it, Fontenot!'' she shouted. "Let him go, please,'' she begged desperately, but Fontenot didn't hear her. His face was purple with rage. One hand tightened around Cody's throat, as the other reached in his pocket for the knife.

"Stop!'' she cried as she heard shots outside the door and the sound of splintering wood. "I swear to God I'll shoot you!''

Oh, hurry! Even as Dana thought the words, she knew the futility of them. The magnetized lock on the door was safe against more than two thousand pounds of force. Fontenot had said so, and she knew he wouldn't have said it if it weren't true. He was too proud of his accomplishments.

She watched, helplessly, as Cody kicked and thrashed, trying to buck the man off him. Fontenot's rage gave him the strength of a superman. He was relentless. He jerked the switchblade out of his pocket and, as he did, the remote control skidded across the floor.

Dana's eyes followed it as it clattered to rest about five feet in front of her.

Cody choked and coughed.

Dana heard the snick of metal against metal as Fontenot flipped open the knife.

Turning her full attention back to Fontenot, she squeezed her finger around the trigger, but her gaze kept wanting to wander to the small black device that, with the press of a button, would open the door for Dev and the New Orleans police.

After what seemed an endless moment of indecision, Dana dropped the gun and dove for the black device, pressing the button desperately.

The door slammed open and police swarmed into the room, just as Cody got his feet under him and heaved with all his might, throwing Fontenot directly into Dev's path as the big detective rushed in, gun at the ready.

Fontenot pushed up and lunged at Dana. Dev swung at him. The force of Dev's blow sent Fontenot backward into Dana's heavy oak sofa table, which collapsed when Fontenot's back hit it.

The madman squealed in pain and Dev sauntered over and laid the barrel of his gun against Fontenot's neck. "Go ahead. Give me an excuse to shoot you."

"You disgusting lout!" Fontenot screamed. "You've broken my back. I'm in agony! Help me!"

"I'll help you right back into prison," Dev growled as uniformed police surrounded Fontenot.

Dana pushed her way through the crowd to Cody. She grabbed him. "Cody, are you okay? Oh, God, look at the blood!"

"Don't worry, *chère,* it's just a flesh wound." Cody grinned at her as one of the uniformed officers helped him up and unlocked the handcuffs.

As soon as his hands were free, Cody reached for Dana with his good arm as he coughed and rubbed the dark red marks on his neck.

Dana grabbed a piece of his ruined shirt and began wiping his chest, where blood seeped from the cuts Fontenot had inflicted.

"See, told you. Just a flesh wound."

Small shivers ran down her spine. "I wanted to kill him, Cody. I really wanted to kill him. There for a minute, I could have blown him away without a second thought."

"I know, *chère,* I felt the same way. You did good. You saved us. I'm so proud of you."

"But he could have killed you, and I couldn't pull the trigger."

"Don't think about it anymore. You did exactly the right thing." Cody's voice was hoarse.

He pulled her close and wrapped his arms around her, so tight she could hardly breathe, which was just tight enough. "If you'd killed him it would have weighed on you for the rest of your life, and I don't want that. I want the rest of our lives to be safe and secure."

Dana pulled her head back to look at Cody. "Our lives? Safe? What do you mean?"

"I think I'm getting too old for this cops-and-robbers stuff."

Hope and fear rose up in Dana's breast, almost choking her. "But, Cody, you love being a cop. I don't want you to hate me because you had to give up your dream."

"I'm not giving up my dream, *chère*. It took me a while to realize it, but being a cop is what I do, my dream is right here in my arms. It's never been quite the same after you left me. Do you realize ever since I've been a cop, you've been there? And when you weren't there anymore to keep me balanced, to give me a safe, secure place to come home to, the excitement and the danger just got old."

"You depended on me for safety, for security? Oh, Cody. I know you love me. I saw it." Her voice cracked and tears welled in her eyes. "I will never forget how you tried to save me. I'll never get over being afraid for you, but I think I can stand anything, as long as I know you love me."

"I don't think you'll ever know how much, *chère*."

But she did know. She would never tell him how heartbreaking it had been to hear his hopeless screams and to watch his desperate struggle to break away from Dev and run into the inferno to save her. It was something she'd keep inside herself, for those lonely nights while she waited for him to come home.

It was her security, knowing how much he loved her.

Cody kissed her, and Dana felt the barriers go down inside her, felt the uninhibited passion that he had always been able to coax from her. Cody Maxwell loved her. There was nothing she couldn't face.

He pulled back and grinned at her. "Let's go home. I've got a surprise for you."

Dana laughed shakily, and tears spilled down her cheeks. "I don't know if I'm up to any more surprises today, Cody."

He kept one arm around her and guided her out of the apartment, around the policemen, and out the door. "I think you might like this one, *chère*," he said as he led her to the car. "There's a rumor that the police chief on Chartres Island is thinking about retiring. Captain Hamilton said he'd put in a good word for me when the job comes open."

"Chartres Island? That tiny little resort island? With nothing but a ferry to connect us to New Orleans? You'll be bored to tears, Cody. Are you sure you want to do that?"

"I'll tell you what I want, *chère*. I want to spend the next fifty years or so coming home to you. And if you're willing, I'd like to get started on a Little League team."

Dana stared up at him. "You want to what?" she asked in bewilderment.

He laughed. "I want to *create* a Little League team. But I'm not getting any younger, so we'd better get started very soon."

Dana didn't even try to stop the flood of tears that coursed down her cheeks. She looked up to find an angelic smile on Cody's face, but behind the smile she saw a trace of apprehension. Just a trace. If she hadn't known him so well she might have missed it.

But she did know him well, so she took his face in her hands and kissed him sweetly, then smiled back at him. "You know, maybe I could eventually get to liking surprises."

Epilogue

Six months later

Dana stood back and looked at the table. The china sparkled, and the glasses shone in the candlelight. Biting her lip, she moved one plate just a bit to the left and smoothed a tiny wrinkle in a napkin.

She glanced up at the clock, and her pulse sped up. Cody would be home in a few minutes. She checked off her list on her fingers. The crawfish were done, the champagne was chilled, and she was dressed...after a fashion.

She pulled at the tail of Cody's Police Academy T-shirt, under which she had on nothing at all. Stifling a nervous giggle, she picked up the two crystal flutes and reached for the champagne, reminding herself that she could only have one glass.

She'd never done anything like this before. She hoped Cody would appreciate it, and not laugh at her.

She heard his key in the front door. Grabbing the champagne bottle, she walked into the living room just as he came in the door.

His gaze met hers and she smiled. ''Hi there, tough

guy,'' she murmured in what she hoped was a sultry voice.

Cody looked shocked, and his face turned pink.

A fluttering panic began in Dana's stomach.

Just then Dev poked his head in. ''Hi there, Mrs. Maxwell. Not expecting company, I see.'' His black eyes ran appreciatively over her bare legs.

''D-Dev...I didn't—''

''Dana, what are you—''

Dana and Cody spoke at the same time, then stopped.

Dev laughed. ''Hey. I can tell when three's a crowd. I believe you two have some celebrating to do. If I remember correctly, you've been married *again* for three months today.''

Dana's face burned as Dev stepped into the living room. She couldn't check on the tail of her T-shirt because her hands were full. She stood perfectly still, legs slightly bent. If Dev had any idea what she had on, or rather *didn't* have on...

Licking her lips, she tried to brandish the champagne bottle without lifting her arm. ''Can I pour you some champagne?''

The big detective shook his head, still laughing, and gave her a hug and a peck on the cheek. ''You're sweet.'' He lowered his voice. ''If you ever get tired of him, you give me a call. I guarantee your tough guy don't know how lucky he is.''

''Oh, trust me, Dev, I know.''

Dev nodded, still looking at Dana. Before he turned to Cody, Dana caught a dark sadness in his gaze.

Dev chucked Cody playfully on the arm. ''You'd better, my man.'' He turned back to wink at Dana. ''Don't forget what I said. Now, I can see you two have some business to conduct, so I'll just be on my way."

"Dev, wait. There's plenty of food. Stay and eat with us."

He looked at Dana, then at Cody, and a look of affection softened the harsh planes of his face. "Not tonight, thanks. Ask me again. Catch you later."

Dana frowned at the door after Dev left. "Cody? Has Dev ever talked to you about himself?"

"What do you mean?" Cody asked, pulling her into the curve of his arms.

Still a bit distracted, Dana lifted her chin as Cody's warm lips traced a line from her ear to her throat. "You know, about his life. That kind of thing. Has he ever been married? Does he date anyone seriously?"

Cody shook his head. "Not really," he said, rather evasively. "Let's not talk about Dev. That's one guy who can take care of himself." He kissed her. "I'd rather hear about what were you offering me earlier." He slid his hands down her back and tugged on the T-shirt. Soon his warm, firm fingers discovered that she didn't have on any underwear.

"Oh, *chère*." His voice was low and gruff. "Let's save the champagne for later." His mouth covered hers in a searing kiss, and his hands began exploring all the wonderful secrets barely hidden by the T-shirt.

Dana closed her eyes and gave herself up to the sensations coaxed from her by her husband, the only man she'd ever loved.

MUCH LATER, THE TWO OF THEM lay on the bed, with Dana's head on Cody's shoulder, as she fed him sips of champagne.

Dana sighed, sated and happy. It was hard to believe

that just six months ago their lives had been put in danger by a deranged madman.

She held the champagne glass over Cody's head and poured champagne into his mouth, missing and dribbling it down his chin. She leaned over and caught the stray drops with her tongue.

Cody laughed. "All this spontaneity is going to take getting used to." He moved his head and caught her mouth with his. "Happy three-month anniversary, my wife," he whispered against her lips. "Want something else to celebrate?"

Dana's breath caught. She swallowed. "As a matter of fact, Cody..."

"*Chère,* guess what?"

"What?" She lifted her head to look at him.

"I got the job."

"You got..."

He nodded. "The police chief job on Chartres Island. I got it, if I want it."

Her heart was thundering like a jackhammer. "D-do you want it?" she asked.

"Oh, yeah," he said, sliding his hand down her hip to her thigh and nibbling on her ear. "I want it. Why wouldn't I?"

She moaned as desire swelled within her. "I just want to be sure you're doing what you want, not just what you think I want."

He held her head between his palms and kissed her sweetly on the mouth. "It's exactly what I want. There's only one thing I can think of that I would like more."

Her face flushed and she lowered her gaze.

"*Chère?* Something wrong?"

She shook her head without looking at him. She

wasn't sure she could meet his eyes right then. She took a deep breath. "Do you still want a Little League team?" Her voice broke.

His body went totally still. Her heart sped up even more.

He leaned up on one elbow. "Are you saying…?"

Finally meeting his gaze, she nodded, and her eyes filled with tears.

"Oh, God," he whispered, then sat up and pulled her across his lap and into his arms. He buried his face in her shoulder, and his embrace was fierce, almost desperate. His body trembled against hers.

"Are you all right?" She held her breath, waiting for him to speak.

After a long moment, he nodded, then lifted his head, and she was awed by the love shimmering along with tears in his clear blue eyes.

"The question is, are you all right?"

She nodded and smiled. "The doctor says I'm doing fine. He said I shouldn't have any problems."

Cody sighed in relief. "Do you have any idea how much I love you?" he asked, pressing his forehead against hers. A tear trickled down his cheek.

She nodded and traced the path of the tear with her fingertip. "Almost as much as I love you." She gave him a watery smile.

"More."

"Cody, don't argue with a lawyer. You know you can't win."

Cody laughed and kissed his wife.

Harlequin truly does
make any time special....
This year we are celebrating
weddings in style!

To help us celebrate, we want you to tell us how wearing the Harlequin wedding gown will make your wedding day special. As the grand prize, Harlequin will offer one lucky bride the chance to **"Walk Down the Aisle" in the Harlequin wedding gown!**

There's more...

For her honeymoon, she and her groom will spend five nights at the **Hyatt Regency Maui.** As part of this five-night honeymoon at the hotel renowned for its romantic attractions, the couple will enjoy a candlelit dinner for two in Swan Court, a sunset sail on the hotel's catamaran, and duet spa treatments.

To enter, please write, in, 250 words or less, how wearing the Harlequin wedding gown will make your wedding day special. The entry will be judged based on its emotionally compelling nature, its originality and creativity, and its sincerity. This contest is open to Canadian and U.S. residents only and to those who are 18 years of age and older. There is no purchase necessary to enter. Void where prohibited. See further contest rules attached. Please send your entry to:

Walk Down the Aisle Contest

In Canada	In U.S.A.
P.O. Box 637	P.O. Box 9076
Fort Erie, Ontario	3010 Walden Ave.
L2A 5X3	Buffalo, NY 14269-9076

You can also enter by visiting www.eHarlequin.com
Win the Harlequin wedding gown and the vacation of a lifetime!
The deadline for entries is October 1, 2001.

HARLEQUIN®
Makes any time special ®

PHWDACONT1